Stealing History

Stealing History

by William D. Andrews

Islandport Press • Frenchboro • New Gloucester

Islandport Press
Auburn Hall, Suite 203
60 Pineland Drive
New Gloucester, Maine 04260
www.islandportpress.com

ISBN: 0-9763231-7-6
Library of Congress Control Number: 2006931642

First edition published in August 2006

Book design by Michelle Lunt/Islandport Press
Book cover design by Karen Hoots/Mad Hooter Design

Also from Islandport Press

Windswept
by Mary Ellen Chase

Shoutin' into the Fog
by Thomas Hanna

down the road a piece: A Storyteller's Guide to Maine
by John McDonald

A Moose and a Lobster Walk into a Bar
by John McDonald

Mary Peters
by Mary Ellen Chase

Silas Crockett
by Mary Ellen Chase

Nine Mile Bridge
by Helen Hamlin

Titus Tidewater
by Suzy Verrier

When I'm With You
by Elizabeth Elder and Leslie Mansmann

In Maine
by John N. Cole

The Cows Are Out! Two Decades on a Maine Dairy Farm
by Trudy Chambers Price

These and other Maine books are available at:
www.islandportpress.com.

Acknowledgments

Mystery readers are uniquely helpful souls, eager to recommend new finds and to talk about what they do and don't like. I'm fortunate to number some of them among my friends, and doubly fortunate that they consented to read and criticize my efforts. Warm thanks to John Jebb, Craig Murphy, Kathy Richardson, Francis Richardson, Linda Russell, and JoAnne Yates. My wife Debby Andrews never reads mysteries and may or may not read this one, but I owe her big time for everything else in my life. At Islandport Press, Amy Canfield has been a consistently supportive and insightful editor—both when we agreed and when we didn't (and she was usually right). My friends at the Bethel Historical Society will, I trust, look in vain in this book to find the Society or themselves, but I owe them thanks for giving me the chance to learn about such an institution and the important role it plays in the life of a small community.

Prologue

Letters.

Why do people write them? They only cause problems. Some of them are valuable, of course. People will pay a lot to own a letter from someone famous, just to get the autograph. Movie stars, presidents, notorious criminals—you can understand why their letters are worth real money. But letters from ordinary people surely don't have much value—except to the writer, or maybe the recipient. Maybe it's good that people have stopped writing letters and now send e-mail instead. It could save a lot of trouble.

But these were real letters, and it was important to get them back. Even if the price was high—not in money, like for celebrity autographs, but in blood: blood on the rug; blood on the leg of the sofa; and so, so much blood on the body. Were these letters worth all that?

They must be if someone was willing to kill for them.

One

Julie Williamson hesitated, weighing the pluses and minuses of making the call. On the plus side: She could talk to her old mentor, hear a familiar voice, get some emotional support, and, of course, find out how much the letter was worth. On the minus side: He might make light of her concerns, and she'd feel silly, as if she were a student again looking for advice, rather than a professional taking action.

Julie didn't think of herself as assertive, but she did consider herself self-confident, a thirty-four-year old not afraid of a challenge. After all, she had taken the job as director of the Ryland Historical Society even though her only experience at a local history museum had been a summer internship during college. However, with her PhD in history and museum studies, the position was a perfect first job out of graduate school—especially since Ryland was only a two-hour drive from the University of Maine in Orono where her boyfriend, Rich, was an assistant professor. Getting to Maine, getting closer to Rich, was a big part of the appeal. She accepted as soon as the job was offered.

So why did she hesitate to call Maurice Leary? Maurice, who worked full-time at a major auction house in New York, commuted to Delaware to teach in the museum program from which Julie had received her degree. She was happy to regard him as her mentor. He would know how much the letter was worth; or if he didn't, he could find out quickly.

She finally dialed Maurice's number.

"Probably $20,000 to $25,000," he said after Julie had posed her question. "More if the content is particularly interesting. I'd have to see it, of course, but an unknown letter from Abraham Lincoln to Hannibal Hamlin would be a nice find. If it's not a fake, of course," he added with a laugh.

The silence at Julie's end of the line alarmed him. "Do you think it might be a fake?" he asked.

"I don't know. The problem is . . . well, the problem is that the letter isn't here. It's missing."

"That does complicate matters, doesn't it? What makes you think it was there in the first place?"

"It's in the inventory. Let me read it to you: 'manuscript letter from Abraham Lincoln to Hannibal Hamlin; three pages; excellent condition—origin apparently not known; very valuable; lock in vault.' "

Leary waited for Julie to continue. "That's it?" he prompted.

"I'm afraid that's it," she said. "Not a very detailed entry, is it?"

"Hardly, but that's not unusual for local historical societies. Where are you again? I'm sorry, I know you told me."

"Ryland, Maine. The Ryland Historical Society."

"Right. That explains the letter. Hamlin was from Maine, wasn't he?"

"From near Ryland, in fact," Julie replied. "A beautiful place called Paris Hill. He was born there. I guess he came back after serving as Lincoln's vice president—but I'm not really sure—I'm still trying to bone up on Maine history."

"All I remember is that he was a Democrat and bolted the party to become a Republican because he was so anti-slavery. But then Lincoln dumped him after one term."

"Right. And then chose Andrew Johnson as his vice president. I remember that from my Civil War history class, but I'm not sure what happened to Hamlin after that."

"Well, maybe your Lincoln letter will reveal all," Maurice said.

"Here's hoping!"

"Now remind me," Maurice continued, "when did you start up there?"

"This is my third day. I hope it gets better."

"For someone like me cooped up here at an auction house in New York, what you're doing sounds wonderful. Local historical societies are fun places, with odd and interesting stuff—like the Lincoln letter. You should be excited to have that."

"If we do," she corrected him.

"Well, there's that. But let's hear a bit more about all this. Then we can decide what to do next."

Julie Williamson couldn't resist the view out her window as they talked. The Ryland Common was truly striking on this early June day—a long green with a Victorian gazebo at one end, benches along the edges, and the big Ryland Inn, white with black shutters and wrapped in long porches, at the upper end. Equally white houses, most of them from the early 1800s and all in tip-top shape, stretched along the far side, below the Inn. Beyond were mountains, yellow-green in the clear light of spring. It really was too much like a picture to seem real—just the kind of place she'd always imagined living.

"The letter," Maurice prompted. "Tell me about it."

"Oh, sorry," Julie said, brushing her light-red hair with a flick of her hand, a nervous habit she was glad Maurice Leary couldn't see since he had criticized her for the mannerism during a seminar presentation her first year in graduate school. She gave him a quick summary. Construction for the Ryland Historical Society's new building addition was planned to begin next year. She wanted to familiarize herself with the collection, especially the valuable items the new facility would provide a safe place for. During the interview process, the trustees cited those valuable items as one of the reasons for the addition—and for hiring a professional director.

"So I wanted to see what was here, to get a sense of how to handle things before the new storage area is ready. The Lincoln letter is supposed to be in the vault, but it's not. It was the first thing I wanted to see, because I'd heard about it during the interview, but when I checked with the librarian we couldn't find it where the inventory said it should be, in the vault."

"Lots of times people move items but forget to change the inventory entry. It's probably just somewhere else. Someone there will know," Maurice said.

"Well, the volunteer who runs the library doesn't. That made me nervous. That's why I wanted to find out how much it's worth. And I also wanted to hear a familiar, reassuring voice."

"I'm flattered. I'll check on recent prices for Lincoln items. But you've got to work with the folks up there, you know," Maurice reminded her gently.

"It's only been three days! I don't know anyone. That's part of the problem."

"Well, you've already talked to the library volunteer. What about your predecessor? I assume you're replacing someone?"

"Worth Harding," Julie said. "He and God started the Society. He was the director for thirty years."

"And a pleasant amateur, I'll bet. How old is he?"

"Amateur, yes; pleasant, well, I'm not so sure," Julie replied. "And I'd say he's in his early sixties because he talked about 'early' retirement. But I don't have the sense he was eager to leave. As far as I can tell, he never had another job. He grew up here, went away to college, came back, started the Society. He's said nice things to me about my professional background, but I'm not sure he's really happy about me having his job."

"Of course he's not! No one enjoys seeing someone else step into his job if the new person has better qualifications. It's natural—especially for men, I have to admit. But that doesn't mean he's not on your side. If he started the place and ran it for so long, he wants to see it succeed. And that means he wants you to succeed. Think of him as your ally."

Julie laughed. "As a matter of fact, I'm having lunch with him shortly to go over the agenda for the trustees meeting on Monday. He's still a trustee, by the way. And, of course, I'm not. I guess I'll have to earn that."

"Who's your board chair?"

"Another friend of God's," Julie answered. "Howard Townsend. He was also a founder of the Society. Retired president of Ryland Savings Bank, retired head of Rotary, retired chairman of the Maine Republican Party, retired first selectman, retired—well, you get the picture."

"Another ally for you, Julie. You've got to make the board chairman your biggest supporter."

"Do you think I should talk to him about the letter?"

"Well, it depends. If it doesn't turn up—and I think it will, sooner or later—then of course you need to alert him. In the meantime, isn't it better to wait and see if you can locate it?"

"You're right. I'm probably jumping the gun. Maybe the letter was just moved, and I'll find it this afternoon; then I'll really feel stupid about calling you."

"Well, I hope you're right about finding the letter, but I hope you don't think it was stupid to call. I'll check recent prices for you. We had a big autograph sale a year or so ago, so I'll start there. Meanwhile, keep me informed. I mean that, Julie."

After she had put down the phone, Julie replayed the conversation and assured herself that calling Maurice Leary really had been a smart thing to do. It would be nice to know the current value of such an important item in the collection, of course, but even more important was her old mentor's advice about establishing relationships with Worth Harding and Howard Townsend. Although she felt well prepared for the technical side of her new job, dealing with people and workplace politics was new to her.

"Sorry to interrupt, Dr. Williamson." Startled, Julie looked up to see Worth Harding himself standing in the door to her office. "I'm probably early," he added.

"Oh, Mr. Harding, I'm sorry. I was just thinking about a phone call."

"It's a great view, isn't it—the Common, the houses, the mountains? I hope you enjoy it as much as I did. And, please, call me Worth."

"Okay, Worth. And I'm Julie. The view really is great. And I feel so honored to be sitting here in your chair. Should we talk here before lunch?"

"I'm an early riser, Julie, so it's . . . let's see, almost eleven-thirty, and I'm ready for lunch. Is that too early for a city girl?"

Julie knew Worth's laugh was meant to signal he was kidding, but she didn't think for a minute that he was.

"Fine with me," she said. "We can talk while we eat. I was up early myself," she added, considering it too minor a lie to worry about under the circumstances.

Two

If you liked greasy burgers and fries or grilled red hot dogs or a classic BLT heavy on the bacon and mayonnaise, then lunch with Worth at the Village Restaurant was perfect. The restaurant, which sat in the shadow of the grand old Ryland Inn, was a throwback. It served the best burgers in town, and the owner—who seemed on a crusade against healthy food, or those trendy foods that people "from away" might eat—was a local legend. As Julie picked at her tuna salad sandwich (also very heavy with mayonnaise, or maybe Miracle Whip) she wished she had ordered something in keeping with the ambiance.

But food wasn't the point of the lunch, Julie reminded herself. The point was the meeting of the board of trustees of the Ryland Historical Society that would occur on Monday. It was Julie's first trustees meeting as director, and Harding's first as, he told her, "a mere trustee."

"It'll be nice not to be in the hot seat," Worth said over their sandwiches, "answering all the stupid little questions, listening to dumb ideas, trying to feign interest in Mary Ellen Swanson's latest inanity, or being grilled by Clif Holdsworth about the peeling paint, or worst of all, having to sit still for Martha Preston's endless babble about the gift shop. Of course I'll have to hear all that crap, but I won't have to pretend for a moment that I care. And I won't have to do anything. Just sit and listen. And maybe ask you a few dumb questions myself."

Worth indulged in the same high-pitched laugh he had used earlier after his comment about Julie's being a city girl. And, as then, Julie knew that nothing was funny. "Wish you had told me about the board meetings before I took the job," she said, and laughed. She wasn't exactly sure how to take this man. Everything in her proper upbringing made respect and deference her first responses. He was, after all, old enough to be her father, and he was a very lean, distinguished-looking man—the picture of a museum director. But he had an odd sense of humor—and a blunt style Julie found hard to reconcile with the little she knew of him. He was quite different from the politically correct world of academia that she'd grown accustomed to over the past half-dozen years.

"Oh, don't pay me any mind, Julie," Worth said. "I like to kid. You'll understand that when you get to know me better. Really, when it comes right down to it, it's a good board. Oh, everything I said a minute ago is true. They all have their hobbyhorses and quirks. What did you expect? Eccentricity blooms in small New England towns about as fast as lupine in the spring. But they're good people and they want the Society to prosper. That's why they wanted a pro like you to run the place."

Thanking him for the compliment delayed Julie from asking about the Lincoln letter, and he quickly turned the conversation back to the board meeting. He really did mean to be helpful. He explained the agenda, who would do and say what, what was expected of her, whom to pay attention to and whom to ignore. It was a pretty good introduction, she realized—just the sort of help Maurice Leary had advised her to seek from the former director. But she didn't get a chance to bring up the letter.

"Separate checks," Worth told the waitress when she brought a single one. The waitress scowled at him, shook her head, and went back to the kitchen. She came back with two checks, and Worth closely examined his before pulling seven dingy dollar bills from his worn leather wallet and handing them to the waitress. Julie was happy she had brought her purse; she had assumed this would be Worth's treat, a welcome-to-Ryland lunch. On a $5.95 bill, the $1.05 Worth was leaving as his tip seemed pretty meager to her, but she felt she had to follow suit.

When the waitress returned quickly with the change, and Worth scooped up the nickel and the dollar and replaced it with three quarters, she decided she just couldn't follow his lead that far. She could tell he was about to say something to her as he examined the change she had left, but she was glad he let it go.

Walking across the Common toward the Ryland Historical Society, Julie willed herself to ignore the Lincoln letter for the time being. Worth said good-bye as he turned right at the far side of the Common and walked toward his house. Julie hadn't had time to thank him for lunch. Well, she thought, if not for the lunch, at least for his information about the upcoming board meeting. That, she decided, was probably enough to expect for now.

Julie came to an abrupt stop as she looked ahead and saw Ryland Historical Society's campus. Its three buildings were lined up along the Common like obedient schoolchildren. They were pictured on the Society's brochure that had been sent to her before her interview. She had memorized their names and descriptions before she'd come for that event. Now it seemed so unreal to be facing the actual structures: to her left, Holder House; Ting House in the middle; and Swanson House on the right. Growing up in southern Ohio and knowing the rest of the country only through history books, Julie had assumed every residence in New England was painted white, but as it turned out, only Swanson was white; the other two were a pale, but very pleasing yellow. Holder, a two-story Greek Revival, was the Society's welcome center and museum, with galleries for rotating exhibits and a gift shop. Ting, also in the Greek Revival style but three stories and grander, was maintained as a period house, with rooms furnished in the style of the 1840s and open for guided tours. Behind Holder and Ting was a long shed, covered with rough siding boards, divided into rooms where staff gave demonstrations of nineteenth-century crafts—spinning and weaving, blacksmithing, cooking. Swanson House was the location of the administrative offices, archives, and library. Like Holder, it had three stories, but it lacked Holder's heavy pediments and other lovely decorative woodwork. Swanson was the newest of the three—built in 1865—and more a country house than a town one. But still, she loved it—after all, it housed the office of the executive director!

As Julie contemplated the scene, two large yellow school buses parked in the lot beside Holder House and disgorged groups of children who were being herded toward the museum by several teachers. I should go greet them, Julie thought—introduce myself, welcome them, show the flag. But the children had snaked into Holder before she could act on the thought, and she decided to take another moment to survey the scene.

Her museum.

Her period house.

Her craft shed.

She felt she needed to give herself the proverbial pinch to see if this was real. A week ago she was packing up her apartment in Delaware in preparation for the move. Now she was in Ryland, Maine, and director of the Ryland Historical Society. A real place, a real job. It still felt like a dream.

"Nice view, isn't it?" The voice came from behind her, and Julie turned to find its source.

"Sure is," she said to Jason Battles, the Society's assistant director. In her rushed first days on the job, Julie hadn't gotten beyond a couple of short conversations with him, but he seemed pleasant enough. "I can hardly believe I'm working here," she added.

"I'm glad you are," Jason replied. "I'm looking forward to having a professional in the job, someone I can learn from."

Jason's face was a little too long and his nose unfortunately looked a bit misplaced for him to be considered handsome, but the smile he offered made Julie think well of him—to say nothing of his compliment.

"That's nice of you to say, but I expect I've got a lot to learn from you. You've been assistant director how long—two years?"

"Three, actually, coming up on four," he corrected her. "Sometimes it seems longer than that, but then in other ways it doesn't seem very long at all. When Worth hired me, I figured I'd stay a year or two and move on. But, Ryland kind of grows on you. It's small enough to be manageable. The architecture's lovely, as you can see, and the Mahoosucs and Androscoggin provide all the recreation you could want. Of course, you can get tired of the small-town thing, but then Portland's only ninety minutes away, and Boston another ninety."

"Sounds great to me," she said. "I'm looking forward to sitting down to discuss your work. I just haven't had much time yet, and with the board meeting coming up on Monday I've got my hands full. But I hope we can get together next week."

"Just let me know. Right now I've got to go and talk to those middle-school kids from New Hampshire about 'Life in nineteenth-century Ryland.' But if you need help with stuff for the board meeting, I'll be back in my office in a half-hour." He gave her that warm smile again and with a quick wave, turned toward Holder House.

When she got to her office, Julie pulled out a yellow legal pad and began making notes about Worth's comments. She always thought better with a pen in hand. She was still having trouble with names, but with the help of a list of trustees, she was able to attach comments to most of them based on Worth's preview. She wouldn't have wanted anyone to see the notes, but she was determined to record as much as possible from Worth's descriptions of the trustees and their "hobbyhorses," and—what had he said?—"eccentricities." Maurice Leary had been right—she should view Worth as an ally. Whether he was or not remained to be seen.

"There's a call for you, Dr. Williamson," Mrs. Detweiller said from where she stood looming in the door to Julie's office. A plump woman somewhere in her fifties, the Society's administrative assistant had a way of filling the doorway. "It's a Mr. O'Brian, and he says he knows you," she added in a tone that suggested she found both facts quite odd.

"Do you ignore all calls, or just mine?" asked the voice on the phone.

"What call?"

"I left a message a couple of hours ago."

"I'm sorry, Rich. Mrs. Detweiller didn't tell me."

"Is that the dragon lady who answers your phone?"

Julie laughed. It was so good to hear Rich's voice that she didn't even care now that the secretary had not given her the earlier message. "I guess even dragon ladies forget to give messages," she said. "What was the message?"

"Nothing I could tell a dragon lady, but I can summarize for you now: I love you, I miss you, and I'm looking forward to spending the weekend with you. How soon will you be here?"

Julie had planned to spend the weekend with Rich in Orono, but now she was feeling overwhelmed by the missing Lincoln letter, the lunch with Worth, and the upcoming board meeting.

"I won't even try to tell you how busy I am or what's happening here, but the trouble is, I'm not sure I can afford to take the weekend off."

"'Can't afford the weekend, or can't afford the time to spend the weekend here?" he asked before she could continue.

"The second one. The drive'll take time, and I really need to do some things here at the office. But I can take some time. Is there any chance that you could . . ."

"I can be there by seven. Will that be a problem? I'll try to stay out of your way—some of the time, at least."

Julie was delighted; the rest of the conversation was short and practical: directions to her rented condo, suggestions about clothing and hiking gear to pack, questions about dinner.

"I'm sorry you have to make the drive, Rich, and I promise I'll reciprocate next weekend. We're going to have to get used to commuting."

"Ryland is a lot closer than Delaware," he said. "At least you're in Maine."

After they ended the conversation, Julie had a hard time refocusing on her notes for the board meeting. She couldn't wait to see Rich. They had met in a seminar her first year of graduate school. It was his second year. She didn't remember much about Jonathan Edwards, the seminar's topic, but she never forgot her first encounter with Rich. He was good-looking—not tall, but with an athlete's body and easy movement. He was self-confident, comfortable in his own skin. And that applied to his mind. He was condescending, at first. It wasn't that he put her down, but he spoke so authoritatively that she felt he was implicitly dismissing her. Julie wasn't easily intimidated, so she fought back, countering his arguments, using her wit to slice into him when he got something wrong. And that proved to be the right approach. When she pushed back, he withdrew, following her lead instead of providing his own.

Still, it was his solidness—she could never think of a better way to describe it—that emerged as the trait she most valued. He had a presence, a *there*-ness that comforted her. One of their graduate-school friends told her that as their relationship developed, Rich had turned into a wimp. But Julie knew how wrong that view was. Yes, he yielded, supported her, always weighed her interests over his own, but he did that not from weakness but from strength. He was so comfortable with himself, physically and intellectually, that he had plenty of room for Julie and her interests in his life.

By the fourth meeting of the seminar, without ever being explicit about it, they began arriving early to talk. By the sixth meeting, they started going off to dinner afterwards. When they celebrated the seminar's conclusion, they did so over dinner at Rich's apartment. Julie spent the night.

That was five years ago, and since then they had experienced their ups and downs, but both knew the relationship was long-term. Marriage was never mentioned. It was not a fit graduate school topic. They had seen too many of their colleagues commit to marriage before finding jobs, and the resulting splits were painful to watch. Julie felt she could wait and see what happened. How long? She hadn't really assessed that, and Rich had never directly raised the issue of marriage. Sometimes, Julie thought, you just had to see what happened. And, as it turned out, what happened was Maine.

A year ago in the spring, Rich—his completed dissertation entitling him to his doctorate—took a job at the University of Maine. The year had tried them, but he made occasional trips to Delaware, and she went to Orono five times. So when the job as director of the Ryland Historical Society was advertised, Julie thought she heard the Fates lecturing her: you'd rather run a historical society than teach; while Maine is a big state and Ryland and Orono aren't exactly twin cities, commuting by car beats US Airways any day; if you're both in the same state, then maybe . . . She never quite felt secure filling in the blank, but when the Fates spoke, Julie listened; and when Ryland Historical Society called, she answered.

They had planned for her to drive to Orono the first weekend, and he would make the trip to Ryland the next, establishing a pattern they imagined would continue until they decided to do something else. Now she was altering the pattern before they'd even started it. Rich had been so good about it that Julie decided she shouldn't fuss. They would have the weekend together. She knew she would have to spend some of the time getting ready for the board meeting on Monday, but they were used to respecting each other's professional lives.

Jason Battles was at the door. How long had he been there? It was spookily like the moment before lunch when Worth had found her daydreaming after her phone conversation with Maurice Leary. Julie hoped Worth and Jason didn't compare notes and conclude that the new director was a space cadet.

"Sorry to interrupt," Jason said. "I finished with the school group and was just putting my stuff away. I wondered if you needed anything for the board meeting on Monday. I'd like to clear out a little early today, if that's okay with you."

"That's fine. I was just going over my notes, as a matter of fact. I think I understand from Worth about what to expect, and I'm planning to use the weekend to prepare. If I have more questions, I'll check in with you Monday morning. You'll be in?" Not that she minded his leaving early today, but she thought it was a good idea to remind him she was the boss.

"Bright and early. I'm an early riser, so I'll be here by seven or seven-thirty. If you have any questions over the weekend, you can call me at home. I'm in the book. I'll be in both days to give tours, but I won't be in my office."

Message received, Julie said to herself.

"I probably won't need to call you, but thanks. Enjoy the weekend."

"You too. Going to hang around Ryland?" Jason asked. Julie had the feeling his question was a mere formality.

"Yes, and really looking forward to it. My boyfriend is coming to visit me for the weekend."

Julie wasn't sure why she added that last point, but she was glad she had: Rich was too big a part of her life to hide him.

Three

Mrs. Detweiller left promptly at four-thirty. Julie guessed that Mrs. Detweiller did everything promptly. She wondered if Mrs. Detweiller had a first name; she had introduced herself to Julie only formally, and Julie had not heard Jason or any of the other staff call her by a different name. But she seemed efficient, and that was all Julie asked.

At lunch, Worth had told her he'd left a large envelope with correspondence, notes, and various items she might find useful. "My transition gift to you," he had said. With the office to herself, Julie decided to explore her "gift." She carried it to the table behind her desk and began to extract its contents. There were letters from schools making reservations for tours; thank-you notes, most in the form of drawings from children who had already taken tours; bills from contractors and vendors of the books and cards and toys sold in the gift shop; budget reports; and newspaper clippings on topics of interest.

On his last day on the job, Worth had apparently gathered every piece of paper left on his desk and tucked them into the envelope. Julie sorted them into categories, creating neat piles on the table, glancing at each item, but resisting the temptation to start working on them until she had established the kind of order that she required.

One of the newspaper clippings, though, was too enticing to ignore. It was a newspaper article from *The Boston Post* headlined THIEVES STEALING HISTORY AROUND NEW ENGLAND. A yellow Post-it gave the date—seven months ago—and Worth's comment: "A big problem. Copies for trustees?"

> Thieves have targeted at least a dozen small-town historical societies across New England in recent months, in some cases walking off with artifacts and artwork worth hundreds of thousands of dollars.
>
> Among the items is a $250,000 Civil War sword stolen from the history museum in Fitchburg, Mass.; an 18th-century tavern sign valued at $100,000, taken from the Portsmouth, N.H., historical society; a collection of Civil War medals stolen from the Winooski, Vt., historical society; and four primitive paintings taken from Newburyport Center for History. Investigations into the thefts are ongoing.
>
> "This is a big loss for us," said Fitchburg museum director Thomas Peters. "That sword was our most valuable piece. And it belonged to the first settler here, so it means a lot to this town."
>
> Police said thefts from small historical societies and history museums are not unusual. The Hudson, N.H., Historical Center, for example, lost a number of maps, diaries and other writings with a total value of $135,000 two years ago. In that case, the materials were returned to the museum after one of its volunteers was arrested and eventually convicted of the theft after he tried to sell the items on eBay. In other similar cases, however, items had been taken by professionals who are paid to go after specific items.

> "Some of these places have collections of considerable value, yet they must rely on volunteers for most, if not all, of their operations," said Tina Meyers, a professor of Massachusetts history at Harvard University.
>
> Sometimes the museums don't realize the value of their own collections. In Brattleboro, Vt., the historical society there was recently surprised to learn that a letter it holds from Revolutionary War hero Ethan Allen to a relative is worth upwards of $25,000.
>
> "We knew it was valuable, of course," said volunteer director Dolores Coombs, "but it wasn't until my son suggested we have it appraised that we learned just how much it was worth. You can be sure we're taking special precautions with it now."

Lucky them, Julie thought—they knew where their valuable letter was. She stopped reading and looked at Worth's note again: "A big problem." Did Worth even know about the Lincoln letter? Of course he did, Julie decided. Did he also know the Lincoln letter wasn't where it was supposed to be? Was *that* the big problem?

Julie looked at the date again. Worth had apparently not considered the topic urgent. But then, why had he included the clipping in his "transition gift"? To warn her about a problem at the Ryland Historical Society? Or because the piece just floated up to the surface when he cleared his desk to ready it for her arrival? She continued reading the article to its end. The other insight she got from the rest of it was that thefts of items from local historical societies seemed to have one of two causes: bad people (thieves), or bad museum practices. And sometimes both, the bad practices—loose controls, inadequate security, poor recordkeeping—making theft easier for bad people.

Julie added *The Post* clipping to the materials on the board meeting she had gathered earlier. It was time to lock up and do the shopping she needed for dinner with Rich.

Julie liked the straightforward name of the one grocery store in town. Ryland Groceries wasn't fancy or evocative, but you knew what they had. She had a great recipe for chicken roasted over leeks that Rich adored. Because he was making the drive unexpectedly, she wanted to fix a special dinner, even though Rich was a serious cook and she ordinarily watched and enjoyed the results. Inside Ryland Groceries she had no trouble locating the chicken. Leeks were, indeed, another matter. She was standing in the vegetable aisle, her eyes searching for the elusive leeks, when she heard a voice behind her.

"Julia Williamson! Welcome to Ryland. You probably don't remember me from the search committee. Mary Ellen Swanson." The tall, erect, gray-haired woman thrust her hand confidently toward Julie.

It would have been hard for Julie to forget Mary Ellen Swanson based on her looks and demeanor alone. She was every inch—and there were a good many of them, all vertical; horizontal inches were obviously not something Swanson would tolerate—a patrician New Englander. But there was another very big reason Julie Williamson remembered the woman: She was the donor of $1 million to the Ryland Historical Society's new building.

"Of course, Mrs. Swanson. I certainly remember you. And it's so nice to see you again."

"You just started this week, right? Lovely. We're so fortunate to attract a young woman of your caliber. I knew from our first interview that you were the one we wanted. Such excellent credentials, so much energy and youth. Just what RHS needs."

"You're very kind, Mrs. Swanson, but I'm the lucky one. I'm really so excited to be here." Just saying it reminded Julie that, despite all the silly worry about the Lincoln letter, she was excited—happy to be a director, happy to be in such a charming New England town, happy to be in Maine.

"Call me Mary Ellen, everyone does," she said. "And I hope I may call you Julia."

Before Julie could point out that she didn't use "Julia," Swanson continued: "I'm so looking forward to our board meeting on Monday. I hope you'll give us a good picture of how you see things, what you're going to do to shake up the old place and move us forward. See you then, Julia."

Mary Ellen Swanson swept off, pushing her cart down the aisle. Julie added asparagus in place of the elusive leeks to her own cart.

Someday, Julie thought, as she put her groceries in the back of her Jetta, I'll be able to just walk here to shop. That day would come when the grand Victorian house Worth lived in was finally deeded to the Historical Society and Julie would live in it, rent-free. That was part of her contract—a big part not merely because the pay was so low, but because she had always dreamed of living in a house like Worth's. The trustees had thought it was a very good idea for Julie to live in the house—once Worth finished the paperwork for handing it over—not so much because its value helped them attract a top-notch candidate at country wages, but because living three doors away from the Society's campus would mean Julie was always available. She recognized that disadvantage, but she still wanted the house.

Worth had told her back in March when the job offer was made that he would be giving the house to the Society and moving to a smaller place outside town that he also owned. But as the time for her arrival in Ryland neared, he had phoned to say that his lawyers were still tinkering with the terms of the deal for tax reasons, and that it was unlikely to be available to her until at least the fall. "Still have lots of stuff to clear out," he had reported, "so it's probably just as well. But we can arrange something for you for the interim."

The something for the interim turned out to be a condo at Topnotch Skiway, the ski area six miles north of town. Condos there were available for practically nothing during the summer months, since winter was the only season that counted at a ski area. So the Society agreed to pay her full rent there until Worth's house became available. It had all been done informally, with nothing in writing—despite Rich's strong caution against informal arrangements. And Julie actually liked the condo. It wasn't the Victorian mansion she dreamed of, but it was large, light and airy, and situated at the base of one of the ski slopes. How noisy and active it would be during ski season Julie could only imagine, but in June it was quiet and beautiful. The only real disadvantage was that she had to drive to work, a task she'd hoped to leave behind when she got to her idyllic New England town. But it was only temporary, and tonight, with Rich coming, it was nice to contemplate a quiet time in the mountains.

One of the problems in a commuting relationship that Julie and Rich had discovered last year was that the moment they were together, both parties had a tendency to tell everything that had happened during the time they were apart. At length. And at the same time. It had taken them a few bad experiences to realize the problem and a few practice ones to develop a routine for handling it. They called it "Your Turn." After the initial hugs and kisses and practical comments about the trip or the weather, the one being visited would say to the one who had made the drive or flight, "Your turn." When that one finished, she or he would say, "Now it's your turn." In about an hour they were usually able to fill in the gaps on both sides in a reasonably orderly way without causing resentment or impatience. And then they would be free to talk about new things. Julie was sorry this Friday evening that Rich would go first. She had so much to tell him, but rules were rules.

At five to seven, as Julie was putting the chicken in the marinade, she saw his white Accord come up the drive and park beside her car. When she opened her door, he held a bouquet of irises in front of his face and asked, "Guess who?"

"Oh, Martin, it's so nice to see you," Julie joked.

"You, too, Nancy," he answered, then removed the flowers and said, "Oh, dear—my mistake."

They embraced, exchanged kisses, let their hands roam on each other. "Any chance you'll invite me in?" Rich asked in his deadpan way that always made Julie laugh.

Inside, sitting by the large window that looked onto the mountain, glasses of white wine in front of them, Rich said, "Your turn."

"Hey," Julie said, "that's my line. You're the traveler."

"But you've had the busy week—new job, new digs. Tell all—rules are made to be broken, aren't they?"

Four

"So who stole it?" Rich asked. They were in bed. Engaged in her recounting of her first few days at the Ryland Historical Society, Julie had forgotten to turn on the oven. It was nearly eight o'clock, and the chicken would take an hour. She apologized and said, "Now it's your turn." But Rich said he'd be happy to wait if she could think of a different way to kill an hour, and with little deliberation she had proposed what they both considered a desirable alternative.

"I'm not sure anyone stole it," she said. "It's just not where it's supposed to be; but as Maurice said, that doesn't mean anything, because historical societies are pretty lax on procedures. It might show up. In fact, I was going to ask if you'd be willing to help me look for it this weekend."

"Be nice to know for sure before your board meeting on Monday."

"Exactly. And this way you could see the Society."

"Indeed it is, and I was just thinking—

"At the Society," she cut him off.

"But if it is missing, do you have a cast of suspects?"

"Suspects isn't exactly the word I'd use, but there are some people I'd like to talk to, starting with Worth. He must know where it is. And then there's Jason, the assistant director. And the volunteers—the board, guides."

"In other words, anyone could have taken it."

"If it's really missing. That's a big if."

"And the roving thieves who go from small town to small town all over New England, heisting valuables from poorly protected museums. Like the story in *The Post*."

"They would have to be on the list, too. But first we have to see if we can find it."

"I'm happy to help, but I hope you're not going to get consumed by this. I do know a little about how your mind works, you know. You just can't resist solving puzzles, can you?"

Julie's interest—Rich said obsession—in puzzles was a matter of frequent kidding between them. Julie always went first for the crossword in *The New York Times*, while Rich was happy to peruse the news sections. In the evenings she frequently brought out a new jigsaw puzzle and tried to lure him into joining her in putting it together. He indulged her by occasionally buying her new and fiendishly complicated ones. Indeed, he had brought her one tonight as a housewarming gift. But he rarely joined her—and she was rarely stumped.

"Well," Rich replied to her confession, "at least you're aware of your sickness. That's the first step toward curing it. But I'm concerned that you're getting too mixed up in this one thing. You should be having fun in your new job, and there must be plenty of stuff to occupy you. This is a big deal, Julie: your first job out of grad school, and you're running the whole damned museum. You shouldn't get consumed by a missing letter."

"I'm not consumed by it, just curious. And getting control over the Society's artifacts—knowing where they are, what they mean, all that—is my job. And think of it, Rich—a lost Lincoln letter! That's just terrible. We might learn something from it, something new about Lincoln and his relationship with Hamlin. It's just such a loss to history. Come on, you're a historian, too!"

"In fact, I'm one hungry historian right now. Let's see if that dinner's ready."

The rain woke them both at around four-fifteen. It started with a sound like a thousand newspapers being swept along a street but within minutes turned to a gentle, but steady, downpour. "Hope it clears for Sunday," Rich said as he rolled to face Julie. "At least we can sleep in today."

After a late breakfast, they drove to town in Julie's car. The rain was still coming down, but rather than spoiling the view it washed the air and made the scene even prettier—the rounded mountains just barely greening, the wide and freshly tilled fields by the Androscoggin, farmhouses—several almost collapsed, several brilliantly restored and gleaming in the rain, and then the town itself, flowing outward from the Common like a group of birds gathering around a feeder.

"It is pretty," Rich admitted as they circled the Common and came to the parking area at the Ryland Historical Society. "Even in the rain," he added. "I can see why it turned you on. You're a sucker for Victorian architecture, and this place looks like a Victorian theme park. How big is it? Ten thousand?"

"Hardly. I checked the last census—3,800. But with the other towns around, it sort of seems bigger. And it's not strictly Victorian," Julie corrected him. A lot of the houses were built in the 1840s and 1850s—mostly Greek Revival."

"I stand corrected. Remember I'm a historian of Puritanism, not architecture. But whatever the style, the houses must have been built when the town was a lot bigger and more prosperous—in the late nineteenth century, I assume."

"Right. It was founded after the Revolution, and a lot of veterans got grants of land in payment for serving. That was when Maine was part of Massachusetts, of course, and Ryland was originally mostly a trading center. But the prosperity came from the woods—logging, and then all kinds of wood-products firms. But that ended in the 1950s or so, and now tourism is the big business."

"From the Skiway?"

"In the winter. Everyone says this place is a mob scene when the skiers descend and the B&Bs and restaurants fill up. I guess there's a fair amount of summer tourism, but you can see it's pretty quiet now."

"That's okay with me. Which is your house, by the way?"

Julie pointed to Worth's large manse up the street from the Society's campus.

"And that is Victorian," she added.

"No wonder they didn't give you much of a salary," he said.

This was a sore spot between them, one Julie would have preferred to avoid. Rich had been her unofficial adviser on the contract and had told her $30,000 was far too low, considering her credentials. She agreed, but she wanted the job, and the free housing—especially in such a large and historic house—was a significant addition. Without rent, she figured she could live pretty well on $30,000, but Rich had argued that she needed to be more realistic about the cost of living in New England, even in a small town. After she accepted the offer, she had told him the topic was closed, but he had brought it up even before now. She decided to ignore it again.

"Do you want the full tour?" Julie asked. "Or shall we just go to my office?" She enjoyed saying that.

"How about a shortened version this time?"

Since on Saturdays the buildings didn't open till noon, Julie deactivated the security system by punching in the numbers she had already memorized and then walked Rich through the exhibit spaces and the gift shop in Holder House. They went on to Ting House, the period museum, and did a quick walk-through there.

"Let's save the craft shed for a dry day," Julie said. "We can go to Swanson House now, and see my office, and the library and archives."

She led him through the small reception area and into her office, which occupied the entire southwest corner of the building.

Windows opened onto the front porch facing the Common and on the side up the street toward Worth's house.

"Pretty impressive," Rich said as he surveyed the room. "You should see what assistant professors get at Orono."

"I have," she reminded him, taking more pride than she knew she ought to in her spacious office. "And don't look too closely." She gestured toward six boxes stacked in the corner. "I haven't really had time to unpack yet and make it my own. It's really just the way Worth left it."

"A museum within a museum," Rich said, laughing.

"Anyway, let's finish the tour of Swanson and come back here."

She pointed out Jason Battles's office behind hers and the small room at the very back of the first floor used by the volunteers. The library and archives room occupied the whole of the second floor. "The third floor is more storage—a real grandmother's attic," she said.

"Probably filled with Lincoln letters and other worthless stuff," Rich said.

"That's where it's supposed to be," she said and pointed to the metal door at the back of the room. "That's the vault."

"Not a very detailed entry," Rich said as he read aloud from the inventory.

"No date, either for the letter or the entry; no note about the content; nothing about the source; no number or code to identify it or where it's located in the vault."

"Don't you wonder what Lincoln would have to say to the guy he dumped from the ticket?" Julie asked. "I can't imagine the inventory doesn't say something about the content—or at least give a date. Maybe it was written before he even selected Hamlin for the 1860 election. It just drives me crazy that we don't know."

"Could be a historical bombshell," Rich added a little more teasingly than Julie liked. "But what's the deal with the chronology?"

"Every year is noted at the top of the page. This one is under 1979, and 1980 comes at the top of the next page, so at least it appears the letter was accessioned in 1979."

"I guess that's a start," Rich said. "Let's see what's in there."

To Julie, the metal door of the vault was menacing. She'd been in her share of museum vaults such as this one, and she hated every minute of it. She was extremely claustrophobic. Just the thought of that heavy door slamming shut on her while she was in there made her sick to her stomach. Still, she steeled herself and turned the key. She swung the door open and gestured to Rich. He knew of her claustrophobia but had none himself; he walked right in and switched on the light.

"Let's see what we've got here," he said.

His fearlessness inspired Julie to follow—after she had propped the vault's door open with a chair pulled over from the library table. It had been easier to enter the vault yesterday morning, when she had first seen the entry in the inventory and had wanted to see the letter itself. The volunteer archivist had been on duty, and several elderly people—genealogists, Julie had assumed—had been at the tables poring over documents. But today, with just the two of them in the otherwise deserted building, Julie felt the need to block the door open.

"Coming?" Rich asked. The door safely blocked, Julie joined him. The vault consisted of shelves on three sides, each bearing boxes labeled alphabetically. "A" was at the top left, and scanning across the three sides Julie noted that the alphabet had been faithfully followed, with one box labeled "X,Y, Z" sitting on the bottom right. "L" was straight ahead, and Rich pulled it out.

"Let's carry it over to the table," Julie said, eager to search the box outside the confines of the vault. As had been the case yesterday, there was no Lincoln letter. In fact, nothing at all associated with the Civil War president.

"Shall we try 'H'?" Rich asked.

"I already did, but let's do it together."

"H" yielded several letters from Hannibal Hamlin—one to his father, another complaining about a bill from a blacksmith in South Paris, and a third that was not really a letter but what appeared to be notes for a political speech or newspaper editorial. Julie had seen these, too.

"How about 'V'?" Rich asked.

"For?"

"Valuable. Isn't that what the inventory note said—very valuable. Maybe someone used the 'V' box for items of great value."

"U" and "V" shared a box but not the letter.

"Okay," Rich said, "maybe we're going at this the wrong way."

"Other than alphabetical, how should we go at it?" Julie asked as they stood at the open door and looked into the vault.

"I don't know—it's just that maybe someone used a code that we don't know about. We're being logical, but if you're eager to protect something that's 'very valuable,' maybe you have another system. Shouldn't we just ask the old director?"

"Yeah, maybe we should just stop, and I'll ask Worth on Monday. That would be simpler."

"But not so much fun," Rich said. "This is a nice puzzle for you."

"But we're not getting anywhere. I think I'll just call Worth at home now and ask him. He could come over and show us, and all this would be settled."

Although Rich pointed out with good humor that this sounded like too logical a solution, he agreed. They locked the vault and returned to Julie's office. There was no answer at Worth's, but she left a message on his answering machine asking him to call her at home that evening.

Five

"I didn't realize you were here," a voice said from the open door to her office.

"Hi, Jason. Just showing off my office. Rich O'Brian, this is Jason Battles, the assistant director."

Jason walked into the room and took Rich's hand. "Welcome to the Ryland Historical Society," he said.

Julie was trying hard to remember something useful about Jason with which to continue the conversation. She knew he was twenty-six and that he had come to Ryland pretty much out of college. "Jason's been here for three years."

"Right—makes me sort of an old-timer, though not as senior as Worth, of course."

"Speaking of Worth," Julie said, "I just tried to call him, but he wasn't home. I left a message."

"Worth went to Boston for the weekend," Jason said.

Boston, that's it, Julie thought. "You're from Boston, aren't you, Jason? So is Rich."

"Actually, I'm from South Boston, but Julie doesn't understand the difference," Rich said. "How about you, Jason?"

"The 'burbs—Chestnut Hill, Newton. We moved a couple of times out that way."

"Isn't Chestnut Hill near South Boston?" Julie asked.

Both men laughed, and Rich explained: "Nothing around Boston is very far from anything else, but in all the ways that matter, Southie is pretty far from Chestnut Hill, though I did go to college there—BC."

"Where did you go, Jason?" Julie asked.

"Williams."

"Williams has a great museum program," Rich said. "Is that how you ended up here?"

"It's more for art museums, but, yeah, I was an art history major and took some museum courses," Jason said.

"Look, I shouldn't be keeping you. I was just going to my office when I heard voices. I was worried because the security system was off when I came in. You mentioned calling Worth—is there something I can help you with?"

"Rich teaches American history at the University of Maine. I wanted to show him the Lincoln letter, but I couldn't find it in the vault."

"Lincoln?" Jason asked, in a tone that Julie heard as a combination of surprise and alarm.

"As in Abraham," Julie said.

"Oh, yeah," Jason said, with a laugh that sounded a bit forced. "I've heard of him." He laughed again. Julie waited for his substantive response. "Isn't it in the vault? Worth showed it to me when I was first hired, but I haven't looked at it since." Then abruptly he asked, "Are you interested in Lincoln, Rich?"

"Not directly," Rich answered. "But I figured I could liven up my course on Monday if I tell students I saw a real Lincoln letter."

"Aren't classes over at Orono?"

"The regular semester, but I'm low enough on the totem pole to have to teach summer session."

"Well, I can probably find the letter if you really want to see it," Jason said, "but it may take a while."

"We've already looked in the likely places—the 'L' box and the 'H' box," said Julie.

" 'Likely' doesn't mean much to Worth," Jason said. "He has his own system. I'd like to talk with you about that, in fact. I have some ideas about organizing our stuff. But that can keep. Why don't I just look around in the vault and see if I can find it? I can leave a message for you to let you know."

Julie gave Jason her phone number and noticed that he repeated the last four digits only. The first three, she realized, were common to everyone in Ryland—a one-exchange town.

Jason left, and Julie motioned to Rich to close her office door behind the other man.

"Should I have introduced you as my boyfriend? I never know what to say in these work situations."

"I don't want to blow your cover here. Jason seems to take an interest in the new director. He was giving you a pretty thorough look-over. Maybe you didn't notice."

"Don't be silly. Jason is years younger, and he works for me."

"Don't protest too much. Maybe you find that off-center nose of his kind of cute," Rich teased.

"Not really." She paused before continuing: "He was sort of funny about the letter, wasn't he? It was as if he needed to be reminded it existed."

"You probably distracted him," Rich said, continuing his teasing.

"Maybe you didn't notice, but the rain has stopped," Julie said abruptly. "How about that hike? We'll stop at my place to change and fix a picnic. I have a plan."

Julie's plan was to hike a section of the Appalachian Trail that passed through the mountains ten miles north of Ryland. When they awoke to rain that morning, she'd feared they would have to forego the hike, but a strong westerly wind had cleared the clouds. The sun was out when they left Swanson House and walked to the parking lot.

"Ryland Historical Society must pay pretty well," Rich said, pointing to a car parked next to Julie's. "A BMW Five Series doesn't come cheap."

"What do you mean?"

"There's nobody else here. That Beemer must be your assistant director's. And I say it's a mighty fancy vehicle for a young guy in a job like his. Of course, he is from Chestnut Hill; maybe Daddy bought it for him."

"And I say you're jealous," Julie added.

"Of his car, yes. But Jason Battles can be jealous of me because of you." He pulled Julie toward him and gave her a big, dramatic kiss. "Eat your heart out, Jason," Rich said, looking back toward Swanson House.

The rain had turned parts of the trail to mud, but Julie and Rich didn't mind. The crisp new air was exhilarating, and after their sedentary weeks they both enjoyed the chance to walk, especially in spectacular scenery. They had their picnic at the top of the trail on a large open area that looked south through the notch. Ryland was dimly visible in the distance.

"Happy?" Rich asked as they ate.

"Very much—about everything," Julie answered. "I'm happy to be living here in this beautiful place, happy to have my job, and especially happy we can do this together."

"Same," Rich said. "At least on the last part. And happy you're living not only in a beautiful place but one that's pretty close to Orono. I'm happy you like your new job; I just hope you don't get consumed by it. Like worrying about the Lincoln letter. You're going to find lots of things wrong, but you have to fix them one at a time. And don't take everything personally."

"You think I'm overreacting?"

"I think you're feeling too responsible. Whatever happened to the letter isn't your fault. And maybe nothing happened to it. Maybe we'll get a call tonight saying it's right there waiting for us to look at tomorrow morning."

"Probably," Julie agreed. "So how fast do you think we can do the trail down to the car?"

She was up and moving before Rich could answer.

A message was waiting for them when they got back to Julie's condo: "Sorry, but I can't locate the letter," Jason reported. "I didn't take the vault apart—didn't really have time—but I looked in the obvious places. I'm sure Worth will know where it is. He'll be home Sunday evening. I'll see you Monday morning. But call if you need anything in the meantime."

"Isn't it strange that Jason seemed so unconcerned and just sort of passed it all off to Worth?" Julie said after they listened to the message.

"He's probably got lots of other stuff to do. Any plans for us for tomorrow?" he asked.

Julie said she would reveal all over dinner. "I made a reservation at an inn one of the trustees runs," she told Rich. "My treat."

Six

Julie didn't think it was possible for a June day to be so perfect—temperatures in the upper-sixties, the air bright and blue, not a cloud in sight. Unfortunately, however, it wasn't the weather she had planned for when she'd suggested to Rich over dinner on Saturday night that they go to church on Sunday, come back to the condo for brunch, and then spend the day there. He had seen through it at once: "So I can unpack for you?"

"We can do it together," Julie had countered. "It's supposed to be rainy and cool—perfect conditions for unpacking."

So the beautiful weather turned out, ironically, to be the first disappointment on Sunday morning. The second was when Julie called the church to check on service times and she discovered that mass was held only Saturday afternoon. Although raised a Lutheran, Julie had accompanied Rich to Roman Catholic services when they were in graduate school, and she found the experience satisfying. Good Irish boy that he was, Rich practiced his faith with a commitment that Julie found attractive, and she was looking forward to attending mass with him in Ryland as a way of making the place feel like home to him—and her.

"Sorry about that," she told him after she listened to the message on the church's answering machine. "No Sunday services. I guess they share a priest with another town and they get him on Saturday."

They spent the morning unpacking and sorting through moving boxes, hanging prints on the walls, distributing clothing. Julie wanted to set up a home office in the extra bedroom, but the absence of bookcases was a deterrent.

"I'm really looking forward to getting Worth Harding's house, but my guess is that it isn't going to happen fast," she told Rich. "Meanwhile, I'd like to make this place as homelike as I can."

"It's getting there," Rich said. And Julie agreed. By mid-afternoon they had emptied all the boxes. They took a walk around the ski area before he had to leave for the drive back to Orono. "I'll be there next weekend," she reminded him as she stood beside his car. "I'm going to try to get away early on Friday."

"Good luck with the board meeting," Rich said as he was pulling away. "Call me tomorrow night and give me a full report. Maybe even read me the Lincoln letter."

Although she was happy with the way she and Rich had arranged her things, the condo seemed very lonely and not at all hers after he had left. She walked around it, rethinking the placement of prints, but finally deciding to leave everything in place. While she was working on the new jigsaw puzzle Rich had brought as a housewarming gift, the phone rang.

"Sorry I missed your call," Worth said. "Decided to use my new free time to visit some friends and museums in Boston for the weekend. You called about the Lincoln letter?"

Julie explained that she had wanted to familiarize herself with the Society's holdings but had been unable to find the Lincoln letter. She also explained about asking Jason.

"Really? That surprises me—Jason knows very well where it is," Worth said sharply, and then paused before adding: "You and I might want to talk about him one of these days when you have time. I can show you the letter tomorrow if it's important."

"I'd certainly like to see it if that's convenient for you."

"Guess your boyfriend would have liked to have seen it, too."

It really is a small town, Julie reminded herself after hanging up.

She arrived at Swanson House at seven-thirty on Monday morning and disarmed the security system to let herself in. She wondered how many people had the code and made a note to discuss this with Worth. It might be a good idea to change it.

How many times could she go over these notes, Julie wondered as she sat at the worktable in her office and reviewed the outline for her report at the afternoon meeting. Even though she hadn't been on the job a full week yet, she wanted to make a strong impression at her first board meeting. She wanted them to know what she was planning to do: a full review of operations, budget, and staff; a planning process to design new exhibits and programs to increase membership and visitors; preparation for the new Swanson Center; and fund-raising to grow the endowment. An ambitious agenda, Julie well understood, but she hadn't come to the Ryland Historical Society to be a piece of furniture. She meant to make her mark.

But enough's enough, she told herself as she practiced for the third time this morning the words she would say under each item on her outline. She settled in to read through the piles of documents she had created from Worth's "transition" folder. When Mrs. Detweiller arrived at nine sharp, Julie was loaded with questions for her. How do bills get paid? Who signs checks? Who answers correspondence? Mrs. Detweiller suggested she join Julie at her worktable and help her go through the documents. It was nearly noon when they finished.

"Has Worth been in this morning?" Julie asked her secretary.

"Not that I noticed, though I've been in here most of the time," Mrs. Detweiller reminded her crisply. "Were you expecting him?"

"He was going to check on a document for me. I'll go see if he's upstairs in the library. And thanks for all your help, Mrs. Detweiller. I'll catch on eventually."

"I'm sure you will, Dr. Williamson," the secretary answered in a tone that conveyed precisely the opposite meaning.

Jason was in the library with Tabitha Preston, a volunteer who supervised the archives and whom Julie had met when she was first trying to locate the Lincoln letter. "No," Jason said, "I haven't seen Worth. But I just got here—I was over giving a tour most of the morning to a garden club from Bangor." Tabitha said Worth had been in earlier, worked in the vault for a while, and then left. "An hour or so ago. And please call me Tabby," she added.

Odd, Julie thought as she went back down to her office. Maybe Worth had heard Julie and Mrs. Detweiller working in her office and decided not to interrupt. She looked forward to sitting quietly at her desk to eat the fruit and yogurt she had brought for lunch. And she looked forward to forgetting about her outline and notes for a while.

At two o'clock Mrs. Detweiller knocked at the office door and put her head in to say that Worth had arrived.

"My own fault," Worth said after telling Julie that his morning in the library and vault had not yielded the Lincoln letter. "I just let the inventory system develop as it wanted. Worked when we didn't have much stuff, but as the collections have grown, while the system hasn't exactly broken down, it certainly doesn't help."

"As best as I can recall, here's what happened," he added. "The letter was given to the Society by a descendant of Hannibal Hamlin. Great-nephew or something. Found it in his house when he was cleaning up to sell the place. Beautiful Cape, lovely wallpaper."

"Hannibal Hamlin's house?" Julie asked.

"No. The descendant's. Have you seen the Hamlin house, by the way?"

Julie explained that she hadn't had time yet to do much exploring. "It's really quite grand," Worth continued, "but then it was added on to quite a bit. You should get down to Paris Hill and take a look. Of course, it's not really the Hannibal Hamlin house. It's the Dr. Cyrus Hamlin house. Dr. Hamlin was Hannibal's father. Hannibal was born there—1809, I think—but when Lincoln dumped him and he returned to Maine, he settled in Bangor. Folks in Paris Hill like to call it the Hannibal Hamlin house, but they're just dead wrong about that."

"And the letter . . . ," Julie prompted.

"Right. The relative found the letter, and he was a member of the Society and decided to give it to us. Very generous. That was in the late 1970s. I knew it was worth something, or would be. So I just entered it in the inventory and then put it in a special box in the vault that I used for valuable items. A steel case with a lock. Double security that way."

And subject to the ravages of heat and humidity and all kinds of bugs and critters, Julie thought.

"Anyway," Worth continued, "I looked for it in the vault this morning, and it wasn't there."

"The lockbox?" Julie asked.

"No. The box was there, but the letter wasn't. Damned nuisance, but I'll find it, don't you worry about that. It's good we've got ourselves a real professional now, Julie; you'll put this place together the right way."

"What's it about anyway—the letter?" Julie asked.

"Not really very interesting, I'm afraid. Been so long since I've read it, I can't remember exactly—something about campaign plans, I think. Or maybe about the cabinet. Yes, I think it mentions some of the people Lincoln was thinking of putting in his cabinet. But maybe I'm confusing it with something else. Frankly, Julie, I'm not sure."

Julie found Worth's ignorance of the letter infuriating. If she had the letter in front of her right now, she would read it and not forget a word of what it said!

"Should we mention this to the board?"

"Today? Oh, I don't see any reason to do that. It'll turn up. I'll come in tomorrow and go through everything upstairs. I don't think the board needs to worry about little things like this. I'm sure they're eager to hear about your plans. All set? Anything I can do?"

Julie assured him she was ready, and he turned and left, leaving Julie pondering whether to raise the letter issue. One of the strongest reasons *not* to was that Worth had been so fast and firm in his response to her question. If she did say something now, she would be putting herself at odds with the former director. Not exactly the best way to get started, she thought. But then, ignoring the loss of a valuable letter didn't constitute a good start, either, she added to herself.

By a quarter to four, when Mrs. Detweiller looked in to remind her that the board meeting began promptly at four, Julie still had not decided what to do.

Seven

The tight-lipped half-smile on Howard Townsend's face, Julie learned much later, was customary—as fixed a part of his appearance as his blazer (blue), shirt (long-sleeved) and tie (striped). But when Julie entered the conference room at Holder House for the board meeting, her experience with the chairman was too limited to allow her to understand that he was not disappointed at anything she had done—just disappointed in general. Howard was talking with Dalton Scott, the trustee at whose Black Crow Inn Julie and Rich had had dinner on Saturday.

"Good afternoon," Howard greeted her with a forced cordiality. Looking at his watch, he added, "I thought Dalton and I might be the only ones who showed up today. I believe you met Mr. Scott during the search process."

"Julie had dinner at the Black Crow on Saturday," Dalton said to Howard.

"And it was excellent," Julie said as she shook hands in turn with both men. "I should have been here earlier," she apologized to Howard.

"Not at all," the chairman answered. "Dalton and I just got in a bit early. Are we expecting a full house?"

"Mrs. Detweiller said so," Julie answered. "At least no one called to cancel."

"Excellent. Good to have everyone here for your first board meeting. Have something?" he asked, gesturing to the table.

Julie took one look at the coffee and cookies and vowed that in the future she would be sure Mrs. Detweiller ordered mineral water and fruit, too. She wasn't a health nut, but Julie just didn't find cookies appealing in the middle of the afternoon. When she was being interviewed for the job in the spring, it seemed like every meeting was accompanied by cookies or brownies or some other vehicle for sugar. It was a New England habit, she had learned, but she wasn't at home enough to adopt it.

"No thanks," she said to Howard's offer. She wondered if she had time to duck back to her office to pick up some water, but decided against it. Leaving now would only compound Howard's obvious disappointment that she had not been there when he arrived.

"Excellent cookies," Howard said as he finished the large Toll House cookie he had been holding while they chatted. "Mrs. Detweiller knows where to get them—a little sugar gives some momentum to a dry meeting," he added, chuckling and wiping the chocolate from his mouth with a napkin. "In that spirit, I might just have another."

As Howard hovered over the tray of cookies, the door to the conference room opened and two women entered. Mary Ellen Swanson was familiar. The second, a woman in her sixties with white hair and of ample proportions, was not.

"Julia," Mary Ellen said, "I'm not sure you've met Martha Preston."

"Very happy to meet you," Julie said as she took the limp hand Martha extended after taking off her white cotton gloves. There was nothing else limp about Martha Preston. Although she was fairly stout, there was a certain taut, tense quality about her that struck Julie at once. She seemed tightly wrapped and edgy, despite the white hair and matronly manner—matronly right down to the gloves, Julie thought. How long had it been since she'd seen women, even women of Martha's age, wearing gloves in the middle of the summer?

"Martha's sister, Tabitha, is our volunteer librarian. Martha runs our gift shop," Mary Ellen said. "Among other things, of course. She's a very active member of our Society, and a devoted board member."

"I'm looking forward to knowing more about the shop," Julie said. "It seems to have some very nice items."

"Not everyone agrees with that," Martha responded sharply. "There are some," she added, looking around the room as if it were inhabited by a braying herd of shop critics, "who feel we don't have enough popular items, but my view is that we need to offer books and educational toys and items not available elsewhere. We're a historical society, after all, not a Wal-Mart, and I like to maintain a certain appropriateness in our inventory."

Julie nodded.

"But I shouldn't burden you with this now," Martha continued, with a sniff. "You haven't even been to the shop yet."

Julie smiled at the jab. "You're on my list, and I'm really looking forward to it," she said with as much enthusiasm as she could feign.

Martha and Mary Ellen moved to the back of the room, joining Howard and Dalton, to survey the offerings on the food table. Julie was arranging her notebook and papers on the long table at the front of the room when the door opened again and Worth entered, accompanied by Clifton Holdsworth. Julie wondered if the trustees followed Noah's ark practice, entering in twos.

"Good afternoon, Worth," she said. "Good to see you again, Mr. Holdsworth."

Clifton Holdsworth had been on the search committee, but Julie hadn't seen him since her interview. She knew he owned the local hardware and lumber store, but she hadn't had the occasion to go there yet. She also knew she didn't care for him.

During the interview, he had been blunt to the point of rudeness, pressing Julie about why she would want to take such a position as director of the Ryland Historical Society. She had felt that his real question was why they would want to hire her for it, implying that her academic credentials and lack of Maine citizenship were individually questionable and, taken together, obvious disqualifications.

"Settling in?" he asked.

"Trying to, but there's so much to learn," Julie replied.

"Didn't think a girl with a PhD would need so much time to get up to speed."

Several possible responses came to Julie's mind, each as barbed as his, but she just smiled.

He seemed satisfied that he had humbled her and abruptly walked away to join the others at the food table, leaving Julie with Worth.

"So you're meeting the crew?" Worth asked, with his usual high-pitched laugh. "Hope my guide to the players was useful."

"Very. But I had forgotten what you said about Martha Preston. She really has a thing about the gift shop, doesn't she?"

"To say the least! But then Martha might be said to have a thing about practically everything. Most folks think she's a little weird and eccentric, and that she also gets all hot and bothered about stuff that isn't really her concern. I've known Martha for years—grew up together here. I guess if you go back a long way with someone, you kind of overlook their faults.

"Anyway," he resumed, looking at his watch, "Howard runs a tight ship. It's five after now, but without Loretta and Henry, he won't want to get started. Howard isn't happy."

Julie's glance at the food table confirmed Worth's comment. Howard had moved away from the others and was alternating his scowl between his watch and the door, looking for the two missing trustees. "Might as well get started," he finally announced. "Our missing colleagues will have to catch up when they get here. Let's be seated."

Everyone moved to the table, where Mrs. Detweiller had placed a stack of paper at each seat. Julie hesitated, unsure of where to sit. "The director customarily sits here, Dr. Williamson," said Howard, pulling out a chair to the right of his at the head of the table. Then he slapped his right hand on the table, intoning, "I call the meeting to order. First order of business—minutes of the May meeting." He doesn't linger over pleasantries, Julie thought. "Motion to approve is in order," the chairman continued.

"So moved," Dalton said.

"Second?" Howard queried.

"A question," Clif interrupted. "The minutes indicate the board went into executive session to vote on the appointment of Dr. Williamson. Shouldn't that discussion be on the record?"

"Don't know," Howard said. "If our solicitor were here, we'd ask him. Is Henry coming, Worth?"

"I'm not the director, Mr. Chairman," Worth responded. "Julie would have the attendance list." He turned to the end of the table and smiled at Julie. "Mrs. Detweiller prepares that, Julie; it should be in your folder—right there."

Julie blushed as she thumbed through the folder the secretary had handed her when she left her office. "Yes, here it is—there's a check after Mr. LaBelle's name, so I guess he's expected."

"Fine," Howard said. "Dalton, would you withdraw your motion to approve the minutes until Henry gets here?"

"Sure, consider it withdrawn," Dalton said. Julie noticed his sly smile and wondered if Dalton, like her, was wondering if this was the board of trustees of the Ryland Historical Society or the United Nations Security Council. She couldn't believe the formality.

"Then we'll hold the approval of the minutes in abeyance and move to the second item on the agenda," Townsend said. "Report of the treasurer—Clif?"

"I assume everyone received my report," Clif began. "You did mail it, Dr. Williamson?"

"I think Mrs. Detweiller mailed the whole package, Mr. Holdsworth," Julie said.

"It's the fourth page, for some reason," Martha remarked as she held up the sheet. "It should be third, behind the minutes," she added.

"Thank you, Martha," Howard said. "Go ahead, Clif."

"Well, as you can see, if you found the report and read it," Clifton said, "the Society remains solvent. For now. I'll just walk you through this."

The door opened, and two persons entered—the first, a woman in her early forties with dark-blond hair held at the back with a bright scarf; the second, a man a few years older and wearing a sharp, dark-blue suit. They were laughing, obviously continuing a conversation.

"Oops, it's detention for us, I guess," the woman said. "Sorry I'm late—a couple of teacher meetings after school."

"Come in, Loretta," Howard said. "You remember Dr. Williamson?"

"Certainly—so glad you're here, Julie. I'm Loretta Cummings. We met during your interview."

Loretta had been a bright spot at her interview. She was, along with Dalton, so much younger than the rest of the board, and her energy and humor were a welcome contrast to the sourness of most of the others. Loretta was the principal of Ryland

Consolidated High School and, Julie remembered, not a Ryland native.

"And Henry LaBelle. Attorney LaBelle," Howard clarified.

"Yes, we met at the interview, too. Good to see you again, Julie," Henry said. Julie nodded. "Sorry we're late," he continued. "My excuse is a long-winded client."

Loretta and Henry took the empty seats at the table.

"Now that you're here, Henry," Howard said, "we can return to the first order of business. There was a question about the minutes. Can you find those—the first sheet under your agenda—and help us out?"

Henry followed the chairman's command. "What's the issue, Howard?" he asked.

Howard explained Clifton's question, and Henry scrutinized the page in front of him before responding. "I don't see a problem," he said. "The vote to hire Julie is properly recorded in the minutes after the mention of the executive session—there's no need to record the discussions in the executive session so long as the final vote is noted. That makes you legal, Julie," he added.

Julie smiled and nodded. She wondered what the private discussion might have been.

"So let's return to the minutes, then," Howard said. "Dalton, would you care to reintroduce your motion to approve?"

"Isn't it on the table?" Clifton asked. "Don't we need a separate motion to move it off the table?"

"Henry?" Howard asked.

"Howard, this isn't the U.S. Congress or even the Maine House of Representatives. Let's just vote."

Howard looked unhappy but bowed slightly to the attorney and then to Dalton, who reintroduced his motion, which was seconded and voted upon.

"So the minutes are approved," Howard said. "Clif, would you resume your treasurer's report, please."

Julie wanted to pay attention as Clifton laboriously read to the group what they had in front of them—lines of figures. But she had gone through the report earlier, several times, and couldn't imagine that heaaring Clifton's patient recitation would change what she had already digested. Instead, as he read on, she surveyed the faces around the table. Townsend, Holdsworth, Harding, Preston, Swanson, Scott, she said to herself—it's like a gathering of the *Mayflower* passengers. Lucky her name was Williamson; maybe she could pass. Only the attorney, Henry LaBelle, had a non-Wasp name. And perhaps Cummings was Irish.

"A motion to approve?" Howard asked.

"Perhaps to accept," Clifton clarified. "I don't think the report has to be approved, does it, Henry?"

"Accept is fine," Henry said. "I so move."

After the second and the vote, Howard picked up his agenda. "Item three," he said, "the report of the director. Worth?"

"You got the wrong guy, Howard," Worth said. "I'm just a lowly trustee now."

"Sorry," Howard said. "Old habits. Dr. Williamson, will you give us your report, please?"

This was the moment Julie had been preparing for—going over and over her notes, rearranging the points, practicing how she would begin, forcing Rich to listen to her rendition several times over the weekend. After almost twenty minutes of parliamentary procedures and the reading of the treasurer's report, Julie was ready to make her mark, to introduce herself to her board as a no-nonsense, take-charge professional. She pulled the three pages of notes she had assembled and, thinking of Maurice

Leary and willing herself not to flick her hair, was about to begin when Martha interrupted.

"Shouldn't we hear from Worth first?" Martha asked, looking at Howard. "He was the director for three of the four weeks since our last meeting, and surely Dr. Williamson can't have much to say about the time before she arrived."

Julie didn't want to meet Howard's eyes and instead glanced along the side of the table. She saw Dalton smiling at her with raised eyebrows and tried hard not to return his look.

"Martha, I think we owe Julie the opportunity to report to us as the director," Worth said. "Besides, I don't have a report prepared." He laughed. "No more writing reports for me. I'm writing a book instead, did I mention that? Some of you might even find yourselves in it. It's my memoir, I guess you'd call it, about my experiences here—growing up in town, my friends, the founding of the Society. It could get downright juicy," he added and turned to look directly at Martha, who quickly looked away. Because her glance was now in Julie's direction, Julie could see that Martha's face was white.

The silence was broken by the chairman. "Interesting, Worth, but I'm sure you'll agree now's not the time . . ."

"Of course not, please go on," Worth said.

"Martha, I agree with Worth. Dr. Williamson, please give us your report."

Martha's interruption and Worth's response had slightly thrown her, but she was proud of how quickly she was able to pick up where she had left off—or where she would have left off if Martha hadn't stopped her before she could begin.

She heard the nervousness in her voice as she began by thanking the board for inviting her to be the director of the Ryland Historical Society and expressing her delight in everything she had seen and heard in her first week on the job. But as she moved through her prepared—her very much overprepared, she knew—remarks, Julie's confidence returned and she spoke with clarity and precision. She realized she had everyone's attention, and she liked that. She spoke about the strengths of the Society, its service to the schoolchildren of rural Maine, its focus as a community resource, the economic benefits it brought to Ryland, its successes in preserving and exhibiting important artifacts of local history. For all this, she noted that Worth and the current trustees deserved much credit, along with the staff and volunteers. Then she looked into the future, especially the opportunities offered by the new Swanson expansion, and the work the board and she would need to do to exploit those opportunities and develop new programs and more outreach.

When she had rehearsed her remarks with Rich, Julie had included at this spot a discussion of planning and a suggested planning process. Rich had objected. Strongly. "Way too early," he had warned her. "Just plant the seed, and come back to the planning process later, when you've got everyone eating out of your hand."

Addressing the trustees now, she silently thanked Rich for his advice; a detailed planning process could come later. Right now, her general remarks were enough—and were, she was happy to see, being well received.

"A lot of this will need to be fleshed out," Julie concluded, "and that's work I look forward to doing with you and the staff and volunteers. Today I wanted to focus on the big picture, and I hope you agree with me that it's a very splendid one. Again, I'm grateful that you've given me the chance to paint that picture with you."

Dalton began the applause. He was quickly joined by the others, some, like Mary Ellen and Loretta, vigorously clapping, others, like Martha and Clif, more restrained, but the whole board was obviously impressed. And Julie was relieved and happy.

"Well, Julie," Howard said as the applause concluded, "I think you can see you've made a real hit here. We're with you, you can be sure."

Perhaps, Julie thought, it wasn't the ringing endorsement she might have had, but Howard's comments were still positive. And, for the first time, he had used her first name.

"Thank you," she said. "I appreciate your support."

"I'm particularly impressed by your comments on planning," Dalton said before Howard could regain control of the agenda. "It's something I've been concerned about since I joined the board last year, and it's really important as we complete the new building—we have to know what we're doing there, and what it will cost, and why. I'd like to hear more about how you propose we proceed."

Before Julie could respond, Howard said, "You're certainly right about that, Dalton, but I think it might be unfair to press Julie just now on the details. Perhaps that's for a later time. We really ought to complete our agenda now."

There were two remaining agenda items: Martha's report on the gift shop, and the open-ended "Other Business." Martha's report, laced with minutiae about which books and cards and craft items were selling and which were not, consumed nearly fifteen minutes when it should have taken two. During it, Julie watched Worth scribbling on the page in front of him. He looked up occasionally at Martha, who ignored him, and then with a funny smile returned to his doodling. Julie concluded that this was probably Worth's time-honored way of dealing with Martha's boring reports. She wondered what kind of relationship the two had had in the past, since it appeared they didn't have much of one now.

"I see we're reaching the magic hour, ladies and gentlemen," Howard said after Martha finally concluded. She offered to answer questions, but before anyone could ask one, the chairman held up his arm to show his watch. "Our custom is to conclude by five, and since that hour has almost arrived, I suggest we defer Dalton's point about planning to the next meeting. If you agree, of course."

"I'll be happy to prepare something on that," Julie said with what she hoped was not discernible disappointment.

"Fine; then I'll entertain a motion for adjournment."

"Just one point, Mr. Chairman," Henry said before Howard could get his motion. "I just noticed this clipping in the material we got today. I haven't had time to read the whole thing, but it's intriguing." Henry held up a copy of *The Boston Post* article on thefts at New England historical societies. Apparently, Julie realized, Mrs. Detweiller had seen Worth's note on it about distributing it to the trustees and had dutifully copied it and included it with the other papers for the meeting.

Henry continued, "I wonder if we shouldn't take a few minutes to discuss it. Thefts from historical societies seem to be a big problem."

Eight

It was certainly not the direction Julie had hoped the meeting would take, but once the news article was pointed out, it couldn't be ignored. Julie had wanted the chance to talk privately about it to Howard, but it was too late now. Howard reluctantly agreed with Henry and suggested the trustees take a few minutes to read the article. The pause gave Julie a chance to consider if she should say anything about the Lincoln letter. She glanced at Worth and was not happy to see the dark look on his face. He wasn't reading—he already knew the content of the story—but he was obviously thinking about it.

One by one, the board members looked up from their reading and looked expectantly at her. "Actually," Julie said, "Worth left the article for me with a note suggesting it be circulated to the board. So maybe he can comment on it."

Worth's quick glance at her was both pained and slightly menacing. Julie knew she had put him on the spot, but it was too late to worry about that.

"Sure," Worth began, the reluctance in his tone obvious to Julie. "This is a matter we've been talking about among historical society directors for some time. I think I've raised it once or twice here. Societies like ours have lots of valuable objects that we often don't protect adequately. That's one of the reasons for the new Swanson building, as you all know—we want to increase our security and our ability to preserve papers and artifacts. I left the story for Julie because I thought she should be aware of some of the problems other historical societies have been having."

"What about RHS, Worth?" asked Loretta. "Are we at risk on this?"

"We're always at risk, Loretta," Worth answered. "Everything we own is at risk from fire, leaking pipes, carelessness, whatever. And theft is always a possibility. As the story says."

"What about our personal liability?" Clif asked. "Henry, aren't we as individuals liable if something valuable is lost or stolen here?"

"There's a long answer and a short answer," the attorney said, "and the short one is that if we exercise reasonable care in our fiduciary duties to secure and protect artifacts and property, we're basically indemnified as a board from any personal liability. That's not to say the Society is fully protected, but I'm just addressing your question about personal liability."

"But coming back to my point," Loretta said. "I'd like to hear about our situation." She turned to Julie. "You've only been on the job for a week. I think Worth is in the best position to tell us about security."

Julie nodded and silently thanked Loretta for keeping the focus on Worth. Would he, she wondered, bring up the Lincoln letter? And if he didn't, should she? Julie's dilemma was short-lived—thanks, improbably enough, to Howard.

"What about the Lincoln letter, Worth?" Howard asked. "I recall you once said that it was probably the most valuable item we have."

"Most valuable *letter*," Worth corrected the chairman. "Some other artifacts—the muskets, for example—are surely more valuable, financially at least."

"The article says an Ethan Allen letter was stolen over in Vermont. What's ours worth?" Loretta asked.

"Never had it appraised," Worth answered. "But it's certainly worth a pretty penny."

"And therefore a target for thieves," Loretta continued. "I assume it's under lock and key."

"Well, now, that's an interesting point," Worth said. Julie couldn't wait to hear how the former director would handle the issue. She saw she wasn't alone; his casual statement got the attention of the others, who were watching and listening to see how he would complete the thought.

"Julie was interested in the letter," he said. "Wanted to show it to a friend of hers over the weekend. In any case, it appears the letter has been misplaced."

Did the silence last a minute, or only a few seconds? Reviewing the scene later, Julie couldn't really say, but whatever its length, the silence that greeted Worth's startling—and so casually expressed—revelation was, as the cliché has it, deafening.

Dalton was the first to speak. "Let me understand this. You say the Lincoln letter, the most valuable one we have, has been misplaced. What exactly does that mean?"

"It means, Dalton, that I don't know where the letter is. As I said, Julie wanted to show it to someone over the weekend—her boyfriend," Worth added gratuitously. "Seems she couldn't put her hands on it in the archive, and she phoned me about it. I looked this morning, and the letter isn't where it should be."

"So it's missing," Dalton interpreted Worth's statement.

"For now, yes. I guess that's what you'd say. But I'm sure it will turn up when we look more carefully."

Julie noted that Clif turned to Mary Ellen Swanson and shook his head. Several similar gestures came from others. But no one spoke until Howard took up his chairman's prerogative.

"This is a serious matter," Howard intoned soberly. "I'm troubled that we found out about it like this, but there it is. We have a duty as board members to ensure that our collections are protected. Julie, what do you suggest?"

She had not been prepared to have the issue directed at her, but her response was quick and simple: "Find the letter."

"Well, of course," Howard said. "But it seems to me this is a bigger issue. After reading that Boston story, I'm deeply concerned. I just hadn't realized that thefts are so common at historical societies, and I for one intend to make sure the Ryland Historical Society isn't going to appear in a future edition of *The Boston Post*.

"It seems to me," he continued, "that we need to do a comprehensive inventory of our holdings to identify the valuable things and make sure we're protecting them. With your permission, Julie, I'd like to ask you to undertake an inventory right away, find out what's valuable and where it is, and advise us on what we need to do to secure things. And Worth, I'd like to call upon you as the former director and current trustee to help with this."

"What about the Lincoln letter?" Dalton asked.

"That should be part of the inventory, of course," Howard replied. "I want to find it, as Julie said, but I also want to make sure we look at the whole security picture. Any objections?"

The likelihood of a trustee objecting to an inventory of valuable items under the circumstances of the newspaper story and Worth's revelation about the missing letter seemed to Julie near impossible. But she hadn't reckoned on Mary Ellen Swanson, who was donating the Society's new addition.

"Aren't we getting ahead of ourselves here, Howard?" Mary Ellen asked. "Worth says the Lincoln letter will turn up. I'm sure he's right. Let's just ask him—and Julia, of course—to look for it and let us know when they find it. We can put it in a safe deposit box at the bank until my new building's completed, and then we'll move the rest of the items there and everything will be fine."

Julie wasn't sure whether to bless Mary Ellen for her stunningly naive statement or to laugh out loud at its absurdity.

"I'm not sure we have a choice, Mary Ellen," Henry said. "Since this matter of thefts has been brought to our attention, and we know there's a problem with at least one valuable item, we wouldn't be doing our fiduciary duty if we ignored the bigger issue while we looked for the Lincoln letter and waited for the new building. So I'll second Howard's motion to direct Julie and Worth to undertake an immediate inventory and report back to the board ASAP."

"Should Jason be involved in that?" Martha asked. "Surely he knows more than Dr. Williamson about our collections. Probably more than Worth does, as a matter of fact."

Julie noticed that Worth gave Martha an odd smile in return for her criticism. "I'd like to add him to the committee, or whatever it is. If Worth doesn't object, of course," she added.

"Why should I, Martha?" Worth asked. "You've already pointed out that he knows more than I do."

"That's fine with me," Henry said before Martha could reply. "Let's direct Julie to do the inventory in consultation with the former director and any other staff or volunteers as she sees fit. That okay, Howard?"

Now Julie liked Henry even more. She had to be in charge of the inventory, and Henry's subtle reworking of Howard's original intention would accomplish that goal.

"All right, then," Howard said, "do I hear a second?" Dalton's arm shot up, and the duly made and seconded motion was quickly voted. Mary Ellen said she felt obliged to abstain but wouldn't vote against it. "I still think we're overreacting," she said in explanation of her abstention.

"Then I think we're heading for adjournment," Howard said. "Let me just add that I trust the inventory will be your highest priority, Julie, and that you'll keep us informed as you proceed. Please call me anytime. I know I speak for the whole board when I say that we want to be helpful."

Julie knew what he meant. She just hoped he was right.

Nine

While they had entered two-by-two in ark fashion, the trustees seemed to Julie to disperse in a cloud, as if someone had waved a wand to vaporize them. Dalton and Loretta both made a point of walking over to Julie to congratulate her on her report, but they, too, were gone by the time she gathered her papers. She saw one large Toll House cookie on the tray at the back of the room and briefly contemplated taking it, but resisted the temptation. She walked alone out of Holder House, past Ting, to her office in Swanson. Across on the Common she saw Worth and Martha. Martha was, as Julie's mother always put it, "talking with her arms." Worth was quiet. Julie felt awkward about watching them and so turned away and entered her building.

Alone in her office, she had the urge to call Rich in Orono but decided to wait until she was home so she could take her shoes off, change to shorts, pour a glass of wine, and relax into a good conversation. She wanted to tell all—the silly parliamentary maneuvers, her well-received report, the discussion of thefts, Worth's odd look, Martha's prickliness, Mary Ellen's abstention from the vote on the inventory, the final motion that gave her authority to conduct it. But she wanted to review all those again on her own before calling Rich. She also wanted to celebrate by indulging. Having been good about not taking the last cookie, she decided to get a pizza for dinner. She phoned the only pizza shop listed in the yellow pages of the Ryland phone book and ordered a medium with onions, mushrooms, and peppers.

The fifteen minutes the boy taking her order had promised turned out to be optimistic. "Another ten minutes," he said when she identified herself at the counter to pick up the pizza. She was about to take a seat to wait when she heard a voice calling to her from one of the booths.

"Julie," Dalton said. "Can you join us?"

With Dalton was a strikingly attractive young woman he introduced as Nickie Bennett. "Nickie runs the ski shop on the access road up to the area," Scott explained. "You pass it on the way to your condo."

Explaining that she was waiting for takeout, Julie declined Dalton's invitation to join them for dinner, but agreed to sit with them until her order was ready. They were drinking beer and awaiting their own order.

"Julie just survived her first meeting of the board of trustees of the Ryland Historical Society," Dalton explained to Nickie. "And I use *survived* deliberately. What did you think, Julie?"

"It was fine. Hard to sort people out the first time, but everyone seemed very involved and helpful."

"Everyone?" Dalton asked and laughed. "You're very discreet. I can say what you can't—some of those folks are fools. Look at Mary Ellen—can you believe anyone would abstain from voting to have an inventory? I don't know what her problem is, but her money seems to give her the right to say and do whatever she likes.

"I was happy to be asked to join the board," he continued, "because it's a good way to get involved with the community, but I haven't been as polite as you. They wanted me to head the building committee because I'm an architect, but I've been going nuts for the past year trying to get Worth and the board to do some serious planning—not about the building itself; that's fine—but about what happens in the building. You just get vague comments from Worth about protecting the artifacts and expanding programming and crap like that. The fact is, Worth Harding hasn't any idea where this is going or how to go there. That's why I was so glad you made planning such a big priority. But now you're stuck with the inventory."

Dalton briefly explained to Nickie about the inventory, leaving out the misplaced Lincoln letter.

"It has to be done," he continued. "But I hope you can get it over with fast and get on to figuring out what this organization is supposed to do. Other than have meetings like this one that turn into a test of who knows the most about Robert's Rules of Order."

Julie laughed. "I did notice that parliamentary procedures seem to be pretty big with the board, but that's okay—it's good to do things right. And the inventory will be a good start to the planning process. Once we find out what we have and where it is, we'll know more about how to proceed with exhibits and programs."

"I hadn't thought of that," Dalton said.

The boy brought a large pizza to the booth, and Julie took the opportunity to excuse herself to go see if hers was ready.

"Let's get together soon," Nickie said to Julie. "I'm sorry we haven't gotten around to welcoming you properly to Ryland, but next time we'll do something a little better than sitting in a booth at the pizza shop."

Julie said she would enjoy that. She liked the way Dalton had conducted himself at the meeting, and she was intrigued that he was an architect; she knew him only as the proprietor of the Black Crow Inn. And Nickie seemed very nice, too.

At home, on the phone with Rich, she described the meeting as succinctly as she could. “Anyway,” she concluded, “we ended up with a motion directing me to do an inventory to identify the valuable items. So now I’ve got authority to really dig into this, find the Lincoln letter and get a handle on the other stuff.”

“But you tried already,” Rich said. “If Worth Harding doesn’t know where it is, how are you going to find it?”

“I’m not sure he doesn’t know. I’m supposed to call on him and Jason Battles for help in this, so at least that will give me the chance to really grill him about it.”

Rich laughed. “I wouldn’t want to be in his shoes when you sit him down with the flashlight and billy club.”

“I was considering being a little more subtle,” Julie said. “At least to start.”

“Sounds like you wowed them,” Rich said. “Are they all eating out of your hand now?”

“Not quite. Clif Holdsworth is a real curmudgeon, and Howard Townsend is pompous but wants to do the right thing. Most of the others were fine. I really liked Loretta Cummings and Henry LaBelle. And Dalton Scott. Martha Preston is very strange—she’s so sour and negative, and there’s something weird about her and Worth.”

“Weird?”

“Well, that’s not very precise, but you just feel this tension, yet they have a strange way of smiling at each other. I just don’t know. But, anyway, Mary Ellen Swanson is another mystery.” Julie explained about the vote on the inventory.

“Think she has something to hide?” Rich asked.

"I hadn't thought so until you mentioned it, but it was kind of odd that she seemed to want to block it. Dalton said she has so much money that the board puts up with her eccentricities. Maybe abstaining from the vote was just that—an eccentricity."

"Maybe," Rich said.

"Sorry," Julie said. "I've been blathering on like this for over an hour. I miss you. I'm looking forward to seeing you Friday."

The two beers Julie had had with her pizza worked nicely with the glass of wine she sipped during the phone call. And having her first board meeting behind her—successfully, she was sure—added to her feeling of ease. She looked at her housewarming puzzle on the coffee table—a fiendishly complex depiction of the solar system. Normally she would have tucked into it, but now she just felt beat. She wasn't used to going to bed at nine-forty-five, but tonight it seemed like a good idea.

She fell immediately into such a deep sleep that the harsh ring of the telephone at first didn't seem to have anything to do with her. After the third ring, she realized what it was, but when she answered, the only reply was silence. She said hello again, and when no one responded, she hung up.

It was after ten-thirty, she noted on her alarm. Julie had moved often enough to recognize that when you take a new phone number, you're likely to be troubled for several weeks by people trying to reach the former possessor of the number, and the telecom companies were getting faster about reassigning numbers. She just wished it wouldn't happen so late. Late! She chuckled to herself; how did it happen that, always a night owl, she now considered ten-thirty late? When the phone rang again, at eleven, she decided to let the machine pick up, but she listened. She wasn't surprised at the silence following her outgoing message. Her machine disengaged before the caller did.

After turning on every light in the place, and checking and rechecking the main door and the sliding-glass door that led to the deck, Julie settled in for a restless night. When she finally roused herself at dawn, she felt silly to have been so unnerved by the hang-up calls. She prescribed for herself a brisk walk, a long shower, and a big breakfast. Although it was only a few minutes after five, the eastern sky was already brightening, and the light was sufficient to quell any anxiety she might have felt about walking alone through the essentially deserted condo complex and up the road to the ski area. She even allowed herself to return via a ski trail through the woods that came in just above her apartment. An hour of good uphill walking and the shower and breakfast elevated her mood. The drive to town was even faster and more beautiful than usual, and when she came up the low hill toward the Common and saw the buildings of the Ryland Historical Society neatly lined up to greet her, the calls had vanished from her mind. This was, after all, the day she'd begin the inventory.

"Worth calls it a double-entry system," Jason explained as he sat with Julie at the worktable in her office. She had summoned him when he arrived at eight, explained without much detail the board discussion and the need to do an inventory, and asked him to explain the system used to catalog the collections.

"Worth developed it," Jason said. "He could explain it better, but I've been using it enough to know that it's simple. But not very good. I think I mentioned we could do a lot better.

But, anyway, it works this way. Someone gives us something and we record the item on a card: description of the item, date, if known, the donor, any special circumstances of the gift like a restriction, and then the location and the date we received the item. Then all the same stuff is written in the chronological file—chronological by the date of receipt. So we can access the item both ways."

Jason's description told Julie nothing she didn't already know. "Who's the we?" Julie asked. "Who does the entries?"

"Mostly Worth, though I've done some, and I guess Tabby has, too. Like I said, it's not very sophisticated, and it really needs to be computerized and cross-referenced so we can locate things. But I guess it works."

"If it did," Julie said sharply, "we wouldn't be looking for the Lincoln letter."

"Is that what we're doing?" Jason asked.

Julie realized she hadn't brought Jason fully into the picture, but she found his offhand response odd. He should be more concerned about the missing letter. But maybe an explanation would help.

"Not just the Lincoln letter," she said. "The board wants me to check everything, to identify valuable items so we can locate them and see what should be done to protect them before the new Swanson wing is built. But of course the Lincoln letter is at the top of the list. So let's start with that."

"Okay; but like I said the other day, I haven't seen the Lincoln letter since the day I came to work here, and I don't really handle the correspondence and other papers. Tabby and Worth do all that."

"I remember. But we do need to get to work, so let's go up."

The library and archives room was still locked, and Jason used his key to let them in. They settled at the table and pulled from the upright case the "L" drawer. Jason brought over the notebook for 1978–1980 that constituted the chronological file.

"You're sure that's the right period?" Julie asked, knowing that the letter was recorded in 1979 but wondering why Jason was so sure that he brought only the one book.

"It was 1979, I'm pretty certain. Remember—I checked for you on Saturday," he answered.

Julie pulled the card for the Lincoln letter from the drawer. "Good memory," she said. "Let's look at the chrono entry."

She and Rich had done all this before, but she was happy to let Jason repeat the process. He seemed entirely practical, glancing back and forth between the card and the chronological entry. "Checks out," he said when he had finished. "Guess the only question is the location—it's supposed to be in the vault, but you've already checked that out. So did I on Saturday. You want to try again?"

They did. With the same result—the letter simply wasn't anywhere logical in the vault, including the special storage box Worth had told her about.

"Anything I can help with?" Tabitha Preston asked as she entered the room and dropped her large pocketbook on her desk. Unlike her sister, Tabby was thin, even gangly—like some sort of bird Julie could not quite identify. Perhaps it was the way she swooped around the room that triggered the avian comparison. Although she was shy and obviously uncomfortable with new people like Julie, Tabby seemed to know her way around the library, and Julie was happy to have help.

Julie explained about the inventory the board had asked her to do, omitting as she had in her account to Jason the details of the board's concerns.

"About time," Tabby said. "I've been telling them that for years—the system just doesn't work. Martha says she's mentioned it to the board, but what do they know about this kind of work? Just a bunch of snobs who think it's great fun to run the place. They don't understand archival work at all, or history, for that matter."

"Well, Tabby," Julie began, not quite sure how to respond to Tabby's outburst, "I'd be very grateful for your help. I know you really understand things here."

Julie remembered now the bird she felt Tabby resembled—a blue heron. Tall and gawky-looking, but not one you'd want to try to get close to because it would flap its large wings and send you running.

"Of course I'll help. Now where should we begin?"

"Actually, Jason and I were looking for the Lincoln letter, the one to Hannibal Hamlin, the one I asked you about last week. It doesn't seem to be in the vault."

"If it's not here, then I imagine Worth keeps it at his house with the rest of the valuables."

"At his house?" Julie asked. "He keeps the valuable items there rather than here in the vault?"

"Most of them," Tabby answered. "Jason?"

"Well, I'm not really as familiar with the archives as you are, Tabby, but it just occurs to me that Worth has a few things at his place that he thinks need special attention. I didn't think that included letters, though—just artifacts, like the muskets."

"What muskets?" Julie asked.

"We've got two Revolutionary War muskets," Jason said. "Actually, they were used in Benedict Arnold's Quebec expedition in 1775. So there's a real Maine connection. Arnold went up the Kennebec to attack Quebec City. Very rough time, and in the end it didn't work, but it's a pretty famous event in Maine history."

"I'm aware of the expedition," she said, sensing that Jason thought he was showing her up with his knowledge of local history. "Wow. That's great to have two muskets that were used by Arnold."

"Well, not by him," Jason corrected her, "but on the expedition. And Worth has a couple that belong to him—not from the expedition, but definitely Revolutionary period, so I think he keeps them all at his place. But letters would belong in the vault. And you already asked him about the Lincoln letter, didn't you?"

Julie didn't want to review with Jason the several attempts she had made to find out more from Worth about the letter. It was not his concern.

"We've talked," she answered noncommittally. And then added, to quickly change the topic, "Would the muskets be in the inventory?"

"Should be," Jason said.

"Certainly," Tabby said with greater assurance. "I think you'll find them in the card drawers under 'M' for muskets, 'R' for Revolutionary War, and 'A' for Arnold."

And she was correct. "So it's not just a double-entry system," Julie said after reading the three identical cards, one titled "Muskets—Revolutionary War period," one "Revolutionary War—muskets," and one "Arnold, Benedict—Quebec Expedition—muskets."

"Not technically—I guess Worth does do some cross-referencing," Jason replied. "I'm sure he can explain."'

"No doubt," Julie said. "Does this mean what I think it means?" At the bottom of the identical cards for the muskets, VAULT was crossed out and beside it were the initials WH and SAFEKEEPING.

Tabby peered at the cards. "Right. Worth took the guns to his house to keep them safe."

Much as she hated to admit it, Julie could see that the inventory wasn't going to get very far in the absence of the former director. He simply knew too much—and could probably save her lots of time as well as a few embarrassments. "I think I should phone Worth and ask him to join us," Julie told the others. "Let's regroup at ten. In the meantime, I guess we should put these cards and notebooks back."

"We certainly should," Tabby agreed. "It's not at all right to have these out and around like this."

She returned the drawers and the notebooks. Julie and Jason went back downstairs.

Julie's call to Worth was answered promptly, and he cheerfully agreed to come over to help. Then she went to Jason's office.

"Enough, but maybe not as much as she thinks," the young man said in reply to Julie's question about what Tabby knew about the collections. "If I wasn't trying to be politically correct, I'd say she's the classic old maid."

Julie winced.

"More politically correct," he said, "she's a retired school librarian, very thorough and dutiful but protective. She considers it her duty to keep everything upstairs away from people with dirty fingers and—sin of sins—ballpoint pens. But she really works hard—she's strictly a volunteer, you know; and as

Worth often says, if we didn't have Tabby we'd have to pay a lot to get someone to do even half as good a job."

"And she's Martha Preston's sister," Julie said.

"Right. Both born here, but they went away to college and work. Always kept the old family place for summers, and then when Tabby retired from her job over on the coast, she moved into the homestead. Martha joined her a year or so later when she retired from some corporate job down in Connecticut or New York, I think. Anyway, Tabby was already volunteering here when Martha came, and she convinced Martha to volunteer at the shop, and then Martha got elected to the board, and it drives Tabby crazy. She thinks she ought to be the Preston representative. I heard Tabby didn't talk to her sister for a month after that, even though they live together and seem to be thick as thieves."

Julie laughed. "What a great small-town story," she said.

"Well, Ryland is a small town," Jason said, but then joined in Julie's laugh. "But to come back to your question, Tabby does know quite a bit about what's upstairs, so if you're wondering if she'll be helpful with the inventory, I'd say yes."

"That's what I was thinking," Julie admitted. "You seem to get along with her. Does Worth?"

"She and Worth seem to work fine together. They've known each other forever, growing up here and all. Although I gather it was Martha and Worth who actually had a relationship."

"Oh?" Julie asked.

"Yeah, but they really go after each other nowadays. I've heard them having huge name-calling fights over little stuff, mostly about the shop. Anyway," Jason concluded, "I get along fine with Tabby, and I don't have too many dealings with Martha, which suits me just fine."

Eleven

At noon, Julie told her three co-workers she would ask Mrs. Detweiller to order in some sandwiches.

"We can't eat here!" Tabby said with deep alarm. "Food and drink are not permitted in the library."

"I was thinking we could eat in my office," Julie said.

"Oh, well, that's your lookout," Tabby said. "It's your office," she added in a tone Julie thought regretful.

The two hours they had worked produced little of interest. They had identified several items of value and verified their presence in the vault. Worth had been candid when Julie asked about the muskets, readily admitting he had moved them to his house after reading the article in *The Post* that mentioned thefts of Revolutionary War arms. He seemed to think it was terribly clever to remove the muskets from the historical society and add them to his own two, which, he assured Julie, were quite secure. Julie told him she'd be over to see the muskets after they'd worked their way through the rest of the cards.

Asking Mrs. Detweiller to get sandwiches turned out to be a bigger challenge than Julie had anticipated. She knew there was at least one deli in Ryland in addition to the pizza shop, which also sold sandwiches, but Mrs. Detweiller professed complete ignorance of such matters. "Mr. Harding never 'sent out' for sandwiches," Mrs. Detweiller told Julie. So Julie walked down the hill to the pizza shop and ordered sandwiches herself.

While she waited for them, she thought about Worth. She felt she was beginning to understand Worth's mind when he explained notes and descriptions on the inventory cards.

Obviously his so-called "system" left a lot to be desired, but he had an instinctive sense of what was important about a letter or a kerosene lamp or a pile of old newspapers—and about the people who gave such gifts. His notations about the donors, usually on the back of the inventory cards, included the kind of genealogical details that showed the significance of the gifts, the way they fit into the pattern of Ryland's history and the lives of the people who had owned them.

One, for example, noted that the donor was the great-nephew of the first man to manage the local train depot. The gift, two lanterns with ATLANTIC & MAINE R.R. painted on them, made sense thanks to Worth's note about the giver. Otherwise, they were just a pair of old lanterns. The family connection explained them, and suggested the pride that the donor must have felt by hanging on to them and then ultimately considering them worthy of being presented to the historical society.

That was the kind of information Julie cherished. It brought history to life, made things fit together as parts of a complex puzzle to produce a picture of the past and the people who inhabited it. This is why Julie had gotten her degree in history to begin with. She was looking forward to working to bring history to life for Ryland and for the visitors to the museum, once the inventory was completed and the puzzle over the missing Lincoln letter worked out. She smiled remembering what she had said to Rich the other night about historians being puzzle-solvers.

After lunch, Julie, Worth, Jason, and Tabby returned to the library and resumed their work. They proceeded alphabetically, and around two-thirty had reached the "K–L" drawer. Since Lincoln was already accounted for—or not accounted for—Julie didn't expect much of interest in these cards, but she was surprised to see a batch of cards under "Ku Klux Klan."

"The Klan?" she asked. "In Maine?"

"Oh, in parts; for a short time, Maine was actually quite a hotbed of KKK activity, mostly in the twenties," Worth said.

"I didn't realize that," Julie said. "I thought Maine was a pretty white state—it sure is now."

"Blacks weren't the focus," Worth explained. "Catholics and Jews were. We had a group right here in Ryland. That's why we have those artifacts."

"Let's see," he continued. "Eighteen cards under the Klan. Most of them are newspaper clippings and so on, but we do have a full Klan uniform, with hood and all. Here's the card."

Julie looked at the description but noticed the donor's name was missing. "How did you get it?" she asked.

"Probably turned up in someone's attic," Worth replied, "and the person didn't want anyone to know his father or uncle or whatever had been a Klansman. But you ought to see it. It's in with the costumes, over in Ting House. Too big for the vault. Want to take a break and go look at it?"

She and Jason did want to see it, but Tabby declined. "I've seen that awful thing several times. Don't need to look at it again. I've got lots of work to do here."

On the third floor of Ting House was a locked room in which the Society kept period costumes—the dresses and vests and trousers and shoes that people simply love to donate and feel sure are worth lots of money. Jason used his master key to let them into the room, and Worth pointed to the racks of clothing.

"Always thought it would be fun to have a Halloween party or something and use these. Sort of a fund-raiser, charge people to rent the clothes for the evening. Most of this is worthless, but the board thinks the people who gave the stuff would be offended. Anyway, here's the Klan outfit."

Worth looked puzzled as he stood before one of the racks. "Thought it was right here," he said. He walked to another rack. "Strange," he said. "I remember seeing it a couple of months ago. Some fellow from UMass was up here doing research on the Klan in Maine and wanted to have a look at it. I must have put it somewhere else after he left."

Fifteen minutes of patient searching confirmed for Julie the truth of Worth's statement that the costume collection was more interesting as the source of a fancy-dress party than for any real historical—let alone financial—value. But patient searching also yielded no Klan outfit.

"This is getting a little embarrassing," Worth said. "You must be thinking that things go missing around here all the time, Julie."

"I'm not sure what to think, Worth. We've got—or actually we don't have—the Lincoln letter, the muskets, and now the Klan outfit."

"Oh, the muskets are at my place. No need to worry about them," Worth reminded her. "Maybe we ought to go over to the house right now so you can at least rule them out."

Julie was on the verge of accepting Worth's offer this time, but she hesitated because she felt that to do so now would look accusatory. In fact, she *was* beginning to feel accusatory, but revealing that right now didn't seem helpful.

Julie decided instead to go back to the library and resume the card-by-card checking. Tabby left—as she explained to Julie she always did—at four o'clock. Julie, Worth, and Jason continued till five-thirty. They had finished the drawers through "P."

"Pretty good work for today," she said, rubbing her neck which had become stiff from poring over the cards. "I think we should knock off. We can finish tomorrow."

The first thing Julie checked when she arrived home was the answering machine. No calls, she was happy to see. Then she did a quick check of doors and windows, which she had reluctantly closed before she'd left that morning. She would have preferred the fresh air from open windows, but after the two phone calls the night before, she hadn't wanted to take any chances. Everything was secure, and she opened the sliding door onto the deck, feeling safe because the deck was a good ten feet above the ground and wasn't accessible except through the apartment. At seven, the light was still bright, and she felt relaxed sitting on the deck with a glass of wine and the phone.

"So now it's the letter, two guns, and a Klan outfit," Rich said after Julie had reviewed the inventory's progress. "This is getting interesting."

"Well, Worth says the muskets are at his house. Unorthodox, to be sure, but let's say that's true. Then it's just the letter and the Klan stuff. I can't imagine something like that would have any value."

"A Klan robe? I'm not so sure. I guess you could check on eBay or something, but there might be a market for that."

"There's a market for everything," Julie said. "But just because something has financial value doesn't mean it was stolen."

"You have to admit, though, that things are getting a little curious. And you haven't finished the inventory."

"No, I think we can wrap it up tomorrow."

"And then?"

"Well, I'll go look at the muskets at Worth's, and whatever else is unaccounted for I'll report to the board, and they can decide what to do. You know, something Worth said about the Klan outfit has been bothering me." She explained about the lack of a donor's name on the card for the Klan robe. "He said probably someone found it in the attic and was embarrassed to let anyone know that their relative had been a Klansman."

"Well, would you want to admit that your grandfather or maybe father had been in the Klan?"

"No, I guess not."

Julie sensed that Rich was beginning to find the inventory a little less than compelling as a topic of conversation, so she asked what he had been doing and listened patiently as he explained a problem he was having with a student in his summer class. When he had finished the story, Rich realized that it was he now who was failing to provide sparkling conversation.

"Anyway," he said, "I shouldn't be boring you with all this. It's hard to be so close, but not together. Even though we're in the same area code, it doesn't seem like we're any less distant than we were before you moved to Maine."

"I know, but I'll be there as soon as I can Friday. We'll wrap up the inventory tomorrow, I'll tell Howard Townsend what we found, then I can catch up on what I should be doing instead of the inventory, and then it's the weekend. I'm really looking forward to it."

After they ended the call, Julie fixed a light dinner. The schedule she had laid out for Rich seemed reasonable. By Friday she'd have this inventory business behind her and be on her way to Orono.

Twelve

Undisturbed by hang-up phone calls, Julie woke early Wednesday morning, refreshed and eager to get to the office. Because a light drizzle was falling, she decided against a walk and arrived at the Ryland Historical Society at seven, laughing to herself once again about the speed with which she was adopting country hours. When she punched in the numbers to disarm the security system on Swanson House, she was reminded that she'd planned to have the code changed. She'd ask Mrs. Detweiller to take care of that. Given the woman's essential refusal to secure sandwiches yesterday, Julie wondered what her response would be, but decided she had to establish her authority at some point.

The inventory team had agreed to meet at nine, so she had time to work through correspondence and paperwork in the interim. Jason and Tabby were assembled at the desk when Julie went up to the library, and Worth arrived a few minutes later.

" 'Q' shouldn't present any problems," Worth observed as they started into the file. "But 'R' will keep us busy," he added. " 'R' is for Ryland, and I think this is the biggest section of the cards."

He was right, but few of the Ryland entries detained them. Most referred to books and newspaper clippings or other miscellaneous items that, while of importance to historians, weren't likely to have much financial value. At her suggestion, they retreated to her office at ten-thirty for coffee.

"When we finish up today maybe you can come over and see the muskets," Worth said as they drank from mugs with RYLAND—MAINE'S PREMIER VICTORIAN VILLAGE emblazoned on them. "You haven't been to my house yet, Julie, and you really ought to see it since you'll be living there as soon as I can get everything cleared up legally on the transfer."

"I'm looking forward to seeing it—and the muskets, of course—but really, Worth, there's no hurry. I'm actually enjoying being out at the Skiway. It's very quiet and relaxing."

"But a bit remote," Worth said. "Especially for a woman on her own. You'll feel safer right here in town."

A sexist comment, Julie thought, or maybe, to be fair, an honestly concerned one. She assured him she felt perfectly safe at the condo.

"Now that's a lovely watercolor," Worth said after they had reassembled at the library table and continued through the "Ryland" entries. "Mary Ellen Swanson donated it. It had been in her husband's family for decades. Painted in 1842. A nice view of the town, very helpful in documenting houses."

"Where is it?" Julie asked, wondering if the watercolor, too, was now hanging in Worth's house.

"In Ting House," Worth said. "In the parlor. Isn't that right, Jason?"

"What does the card say?" Jason asked.

"Ting, of course. But you see it when you give tours, don't you?"

"I know the one you mean," Jason said, "but I don't include it in my tour, so I really don't pay that much attention to it."

"Well, if there's a question, I think we ought to verify it," Julie said. "Wouldn't an 1842 painting be worth something?"

"Certainly," Worth said. "Five or six thousand, I'd guess—it's not a typical primitive, and though it's not signed, I'm sure it's by an identifiable artist. Old paintings always fetch a high price at auctions these days. Let's go check."

"Not that one," Worth said as he, Julie, and Jason stood in front of the framed view of Ryland hanging over the mantle in the parlor at Ting House. "That's a litho of an advertising piece done for the railroad."

Julie sensed Worth's agitation. He went out to look for the volunteer guide who worked in Ting House and came back with her. "Louise Danners," Worth introduced the woman to Julie. "I think we put it up in April, maybe early May," Louise said. "We noticed the other one had been moved and decided to bring this one in from the hall. I hope that was okay, Worth."

"I didn't know a thing about it," said Jason, looking darkly at the volunteer, who was blushing.

"Well, don't you worry, Louise," Worth said soothingly. "I'm sure it will turn up." He dismissed Louise Danners, who sheepishly backed out of the room.

"This is wrong, Jason," Worth said, turning on the young man. "It's your job to make sure changes are reported and recorded. Didn't you notice the watercolor was missing?"

"Obviously not, or I would certainly have said something. The tours get to be pretty routine, and you sort of go on automatic pilot. I guess I just missed it."

Julie was no less happy than Worth about Jason's failure to note the missing watercolor, but she didn't think that standing in the parlor offered the most professional setting for berating the young man. She would have a talk with him later. The key thing was that another item was missing—a potentially valuable painting.

"Worth, the important thing right now is to see if the painting is somewhere else. Jason, would you please walk through every room of all the buildings, and ask all the volunteers. I want to be sure."

Jason sulked off, obviously not pleased with either Worth's criticism or Julie's order.

"We'll be in the library. Join us when you're done," Julie said.

Walking back to Swanson House, Worth said, "Julie, it's my fault for not talking to you about Jason before this. I intended to find a better time to sit down with you and discuss him, so don't think this is just because of the painting. It's typical, though. I have concerns about this young man. Can we go into your office?"

His question didn't seem to allow anything other than a positive response. When they were seated at the worktable, Worth began.

"I hired him, of course, and I still don't regret that. He's bright and hardworking—really wants to make a career of this. In fact—I don't know if you're aware of this—he applied for the director's job. But if he had asked me first, I would have discouraged him. He's not ready for it; he doesn't have the maturity to run the place. Jason has a certain lifestyle that isn't compatible with the responsibilities of this job."

"Lifestyle?" Julie asked. "I don't know what you mean."

"Well, for one thing, as they say in the country, he's got more dollars than sense. He likes expensive things, and the good life."

"Like his car?"

"You noticed? That's one thing—you don't see too many employees of small-town historical societies running around in a BMW. And he owns a very nice little Cape over in East Ryland. Fixed it up—quite a good restoration, but, well, just a little *too* good, if you know what I mean. And his friends, they're a problem, too. Young people—boys and girls—come up on the weekend from Boston and New York and who knows where. Sometimes four or five at a time. And not just weekends; some of them stay a week or two. Skiers, probably, but it just doesn't fit the local habits, I'm afraid. He's not very professional in his off-hours."

Julie found Worth's description of Jason's friends as "boys and girls" funny, but she realized he was quite serious in his concerns.

"It's not really my business," Worth continued, "but his lifestyle isn't good for the reputation of the Society. Maine is a live-and-let-live place, but this is a small town, Julie, and people know other people's business. Jason and his pals go to the Green Roof—that terrible place on Chapman Street—and drink to all hours of the morning. Do you know the Green Roof? I'd advise you to stay away from it.

"Now his work is acceptable," Worth continued before Julie could respond about the Green Roof or ask what harm drinking there did.

"Not the best, but he is very dedicated and works hard. He's in here at all hours, doing whatever is needed. But he's not careful—like this picture business. He should have noted that immediately and taken the initiative to find out what happened. But as you could see, he was pretty casual about it even now. I still think he has a lot of potential, and I was hoping that working for you would help him. I've taught him whatever I can, but he needs to take another step. Well, that's really what I wanted to say to you about Jason, and I'm sorry about the timing."

Julie wondered just how sorry Worth really was about the timing. Was this his subtle way of pointing an accusing finger at the young man? Hadn't Worth been "pretty casual" about things himself? Jason apparently had means inconsistent with his historical society salary, and he led a life that depended on those means. Might he be supplementing his income with occasional thefts from the Society? Or might the "boys and girls" who visited him have larcenous tendencies? Was that what Worth was trying to tell her? Either way, the situation had suddenly become more complicated.

"I appreciate the information, Worth," Julie said with a tone that she hoped would convey her desire to end the discussion. "I really haven't had a chance to talk to Jason indepth yet, and I really need to do that. But thanks for your insights. Why don't we meet back upstairs after lunch, say one-thirty?"

Jason came to the door of Julie's office a little after one. "No luck, I'm sorry to say," he reported. "I can't find it anywhere, and none of the volunteers knows where it is. The woman who helped Louise Danners substitute the lithograph said she thinks it was late April when they noticed the watercolor was missing. Of course they should have told me, and of course I should have noticed. I'm sorry, Julie. I apologize. Is there anything I can do?"

She wanted to say the obvious—that he could find the watercolor, and keep looking until he did—but that seemed pointless.

"The way this is going, Jason," she said instead, "I think we just need to finish the inventory and get a full list of what's missing and proceed from there. We can talk about what happened in Ting House later."

She wanted to give herself ample opportunity to come back to Jason's conduct, but first she wanted to get the inventory over and done with—whatever the results it yielded.

"You know all about these," Tabby said to Jason as the team started the "Y" file. "The Brigham Young correspondence," she added for Julie's sake. "Jason's been working on those letters the last few months."

"Longer than that," Jason said. "I'm doing a little research project," he explained to Julie.

"I didn't know there was a Mormon connection in Ryland," Julie said, regretting that this was the second time in two days she had revealed her ignorance of local history—first about the Klan, and now about the Mormon leader Brigham Young.

"Oh, yes," Worth began before Jason could respond. "Brigham Young actually preached here—over in West Ryland. Spent several weeks in the area, and developed quite a little group of followers. Those are the ones who wrote the letters."

"So they're letters *to* Brigham Young," Julie said.

"And from," Worth said. "It's a nice sampling—what, Jason, about fifteen letters or so in all?"

"Five from Young, and eight from others to him—thirteen total," Jason said. "I figured there's an article in that since, like you, Julie, most people don't know about Young's work around here. Everyone associates him with Utah, but his early missionizing around Maine was pretty successful. He got a couple of families from West Ryland to follow him. It's pretty interesting stuff."

"Sounds like it," Julie said, "but the letters—they're in the vault?"

"Yes. As Tabby said, I've been working on them. Used them about two weeks ago, I think. Look under 'Y,' " he added needlessly as Julie got up and entered the vault. She pulled out the "Y" box and brought it back to the table. Jason carefully leafed through the papers. The rest sat silently, watching. Jason started at the front again. Reaching the end of the box, he said, "I don't believe this."

"Don't tell me," Julie said.

"Let's check 'M' for Mormon."

"So they're missing," Julie said firmly after Jason had unsuccessfully gone through the "M" box.

"Jason, didn't you take those down to your office to work on?" Tabitha Preston asked.

"Just once. I shouldn't have, but I wanted to verify the wording against the text on my computer. I should have printed it out and brought it up here, but it was easier to take the letters down to the office. But I brought them back—you saw that, Tabby."

"Yes, I did. It was a little unorthodox, but seeing as Jason is the assistant director, what could I say? And I did confirm that he returned them to this box. He wanted me to do that."

"I don't think Jason's carrying the letters to his office is a problem we ought to be concerned with now," Julie said. "What we need to do is find the letters. Let me just go through this box to be sure. And, Worth, why don't you take the boxes just before and after 'Y'—in case the correspondence was misfiled."

Fifteen minutes later, Julie sighed and said, "Okay, we'll add the Brigham Young correspondence to the list of the missing. Surely 'Z' won't take us too long."

"So the muskets are the last things to check," Julie said to Worth as they sat in her office. She had sent Jason and Tabby home after they finished the last of the card drawers. Worth had accompanied her to her office.

"Let's do it now," Worth said. "I'm sure you want to get this finished."

Worth's house was a few doors south of the Society's property, on the main street. Unlike the three RHS properties, Worth's was high Victorian. No one who valued symmetry could love it, but Julie's taste was eclectic—so long as a building was old.

"Built in 1883," Worth said as they stood in front of it. "Nothing's been added, but I've tried to keep it up as best I could, making sure the colors were right when I repainted, keeping all the fenestration, and so forth."

"It's charming," Julie said. "I love that section with the turret and the windows, and the porch is wonderful."

"Before air-conditioning, the builders knew what they were doing with long porches under deep overhangs," Worth said. "Nice cool spot on a hot summer evening—and the house itself stays cooler because those overhangs keep out the sun."

They walked up the steps to the porch and entered the front door. "Of course in a Colonial or Federal building, no New Englander in his right mind would use the front door," Worth observed. "But this kind of house was meant to be entered grandly. Look." He opened the door, and Julie found herself staring into a very large entrance foyer. Off it to the left were entrances into other rooms; on the right was the living room.

"These pocket doors would normally have been closed," Worth said, "but I like some circulation—and I like seeing into the other rooms from here. Come in," he said. "The muskets are back behind this room." He led her through the door into the second room on the left. "It was the 'back parlor,' " Worth said. "Sort of like a family room today—less formal than the big parlor on the other side, and a place where the family would gather privately.

"I keep the muskets in here," he continued as he advanced to a set of two high doors. Hard to know what the original owners used it for—games, photo albums, stereopticons, whatever. Stuff for the family to use. Seemed like a safe place to keep valuables."

Worth took a ring of keys from his pocket and inserted one, a long skeleton key, into the lock hole on the left cabinet and then into the right one. He grasped the handles of both doors simultaneously to pull them open. Julie thought he looked like a magician about to reveal his cabinet of secrets. He stepped back as the two doors opened.

The cabinet was empty.

Thirteen

"I can't believe it!" Worth exclaimed as he and Julie gazed at the empty cabinet.

"Why not?" Julie asked more sharply than she later wished she had. "You've had enough practice."

Worth looked dumbly at her, then back at the empty cabinet.

"This just isn't possible," Worth finally said. "The two family pieces have been here since I've owned the house, and I figured the two from the Society would be safe with them. I just can't believe they're gone."

"Is there any chance you put them somewhere else?"

"No. These locked cabinets are perfect for them. At least I thought so."

Worth retreated from his spot in front of the cabinet and lowered himself to a daybed beside the window. Julie thought he looked truly dazed, as if he had hit his head on a low beam and temporarily lost consciousness. He now looked more like he was seventy-five rather than in his early sixties, as Julie assumed he was. "I don't know what to tell you," he said in a low, sad voice. "The Lincoln letter, the painting, the Klan robe, the Brigham Young correspondence—now this!"

Julie's fear was now confirmed. The Ryland Historical Society had been ripped off. Valuable artifacts had been stolen—by someone, somehow, sometime.

"Worth, I think I'd better call Howard Townsend right away. I'm sure you'll want to report the loss of your own guns, too, but let me call Mr. Townsend first and see what he thinks we should do."

Worth seemed in no state to object or to seize the initiative himself. "Whatever you think. You can call Howard from here if you like."

"I'll go to my office. I'll let you know what he says."

Worth meekly agreed. She made the brief walk to Swanson House and let herself in. She hadn't set the security code when they left to go to Worth's, nor, apparently, had Jason, but the door was locked, and she used her key to enter the building. Howard answered his phone promptly. The shock was evident in his voice when, after Julie briefly summarized the losses, he said, "This is just tragic. Nothing like this has ever happened before. We've got to act quickly to report the losses."

"To?" Julie asked.

"Well, the board of trustees, first, of course; they need to know. Then the insurance company and, I suppose, the police."

Julie agreed. Howard said he would take care of the trustees if she would see to the insurance and the police. Then he reconsidered: "Maybe I should come along with you to see the chief. I'm chairman of the board, after all, and Mike will expect me to be involved."

"Mike?"

"Mike Barlow, our chief of police. Yes, I think we should see him together. Is Worth with you?"

"He's at home, but I told him I'd go back after I talked to you."

"Fine. He should come with us. After all, two of the muskets are his personal property. I'll call Mike and see if we can meet with him. If you don't hear from me otherwise, assume we'll meet at seven at your office. And I'll start calling the trustees as soon as I finish my supper."

"Sorry I interrupted," Julie said.

"Think nothing of it."

Julie waited several minutes just to be sure Howard didn't call back, then walked to Worth's house to inform him. It was almost six. Julie felt she needed to eat but wasn't inclined to invite Worth to join her. He still seemed stunned, but he agreed to come to her office at seven. Julie walked down the hill to the pizza shop to buy herself a sandwich, which she ate at her desk. Then she made a list of the missing items and looked through the insurance file in Mrs. Detweiller's office to find out who the Society's carrier was and what needed to be done to notify them of the losses. She wasn't surprised that the policy was from LaBelle Insurance. Julie knew it was common for lawyers to sell insurance and real estate and whatever else it took to earn a living out of a small-town practice. Since she liked Henry LaBelle, she was relieved that he would be the one she would have to deal with on this. The chief of police was another matter; she hadn't even heard his name before.

A tall dark-haired man about her age was standing at the door to her office. "Mike Barlow," he said as he extended his hand to Julie.

"Julie Williamson," she replied.

"Sorry we haven't met before. Welcome to Ryland. It's a safe and quiet little town, as you've already discovered."

It wasn't exactly a wink that he gave her, but it was close enough, and Julie felt immediately relieved and calmed by the policeman.

"Or maybe safe isn't quite the right word," he said. "Understand you've had some thefts."

Neither Howard nor Worth had arrived yet, but Julie felt no hesitation in telling the chief about the missing items. She started by handing him the list she had made. He scrutinized it as she began to explain the circumstances of discovering the losses.

"Evening, Mike, Julie," Howard said as he entered Julie's office, followed by Worth.

"I just gave Chief Barlow a list of the missing items," Julie said.

"Do you know why we asked for the inventory to begin with, Mike?" Howard asked. He asked Julie if she had a copy of *The Post* article handy. Julie extracted the clipping from the pile of papers on her desk and handed it to the police chief. He glanced through it quickly. "I'm afraid that I'm not as familiar with the Ryland Historical Society as I should be. Didn't realize you had such valuable stuff. Let me just get a few things straight."

He opened the folder he was carrying and began to take notes. Howard told him about the board meeting on Monday and the decision to undertake an inventory.

"For any particular reason?" the chief asked. "Or just because of the story?"

"Well, just in general," Howard replied. "Because of the story, really."

"And the Lincoln letter," Julie added. "We already knew about that."

Worth was silent, but Julie couldn't decide if it was because he was still dazed about the muskets or if he didn't want the letter brought up. Julie went on to explain to the policeman about how she had looked for the Lincoln letter before the board meeting and then had brought it up after the discussion the news story had inspired.

"So you decided to wait to report the missing letter until you had checked everything else?" the chief asked.

"We thought that was the right thing to do, Mike," Howard said. "Get a full picture—we felt, some of us, that the Lincoln letter would probably show up when they started checking everything."

"Must be pretty valuable," Mike said. "A letter from Abraham Lincoln. How much is it worth?"

"The letter wasn't appraised," Julie said, "but I did a little checking, and it could be worth $20,000. Maybe more."

"Worth stealing. How about the other items here?" Mike picked up the handwritten list Julie had given him. "The painting, for example. Any guess on that?"

"The fact is, as Howard said," Julie answered, "we don't have appraisals on these items. At least as far as I know." Worth nodded but still said nothing.

"But you have insurance?" Mike asked.

"Of course. That's part of our job," Howard said. "As a board, we have a responsibility to insure the Society's holdings."

"So there's an appraisal somewhere," Mike said. "I assume the insurance policy would require that."

"Well, I'm not sure," Worth said. "Henry LaBelle took care of the insurance, but I don't recall having any particular appraisal."

"Just general coverage?" Mike asked. "No scheduled items?"

"I'm not sure I follow," Worth said.

"Scheduled items—most policies I've had to deal with require a separate list, a schedule, of items of particular value—jewelry, antiques, that kind of thing. But I can check with

Henry on that." Mike made another note on his pad. "Does he know about this?"

"I called him," Howard said. "Wanted to let the full board know about this, but I didn't get to everyone. I did leave a message for Henry, though, so he'll know soon enough."

"Good," Mike said. "I'll give him a call, too. Now, let's get back to this inventory. Julie, tell me what you did and how you found these things—or didn't find them, I guess I should say."

Julie explained the nature of the inventory, the way the system worked, what she and Worth, Jason and Tabby had done. Mike continued to take notes, occasionally interrupting her to clarify a point.

"Well," he said when she had carried the story up through the discovery of the missing muskets at Worth Harding's house just a few hours ago, "I guess I've got enough to get started on. I'll put this out on the system, notify other law enforcement agencies about the items. You'd be surprised," he said, addressing Julie directly, "how quickly things turn up at pawn shops or antique stores after we put them on the alert list."

"I hope so," Howard said before Julie could reply. "But do we have to say anything about the Society, Mike?"

"Have to say who owns the items, when and where they might have been stolen. That's standard, Howard."

"I see. My concern is that we don't want to alarm folks. We're still raising money for the campaign, and if people think we don't take care of our holdings, they might not be inclined to support us. I just want to be careful."

"Trying to recover the items is the most important thing, isn't it?" Mike asked.

Howard's agreement struck Julie as less than wholehearted. For him, Julie recognized, the reputation of the Ryland Historical Society trumped its artifacts.

"I'll keep you informed," Mike said to Julie as he left.

She appreciated that his comment was directed to her rather than Howard or Worth. "Thanks. And I'll let you know if anything develops here."

"I'm thinking we need a special meeting of the board to address this," Howard said as he rose to leave. "Friday. We should know more by then. Let's say four on Friday. Would you have Mrs. Detweiller call everyone tomorrow?"

Four o'clock Friday? The exact time she had expected to be on the road to Orono. Oh well, it couldn't be helped. She sighed. Taking the job had seemed so right and so simple. But now she was in over her head. All her academic training was fine for the technical side of the job—a side, she realized, she had barely addressed—but it hadn't really provided the sort of real-world skills she knew she needed to deal with Howard Townsend. And Jason Battles, too. Maybe even Mrs. Detweiller.

I've got to be more assertive, Julie told herself. And I will. Now that, she said to herself as she left the building, is assertiveness!

Fourteen

Although distant and muffled, the sound was obviously a ringing telephone. If she ran, Julie could get up the stairs, unlock and open the front door, and sprint to the kitchen to reach it in time. She did just that.

"Hello," she said, breathlessly.

No response.

"Hello," she repeated.

Still nothing.

"Cut the crap, asshole," she shouted. "If you have something to say, say it. Otherwise, stop this, or you'll be sorry. Okay? Good-bye."

She slammed the receiver onto the cradle.

Brave talk, she thought, but she didn't feel brave. She walked through the condo, checking windows and the door to the deck. She ended back at the front door, left slightly ajar when she rushed in. She pulled it shut, turned the lock and headed back to the kitchen, this time to make a call of her own.

"Rich, I'm sorry but I have bad news about the weekend. I can't come to Orono. I hope you can come here. Give me a call as soon as you can so I can explain. I love you."

Julie hoped the message she left on Rich's answering machine wasn't too brusque, but she was just so angry. She was angry at Worth's carelessness; angry that Howard had scheduled the special board meeting without discussing it with her; angry that he set a time that interfered with her weekend plan; angry that her dream job wasn't going quite as planned. And she was angry that some jerk was harassing her with hang-up calls.

"Okay, jerk," she said out loud when the phone rang again, interrupting her catalog of angers. "What do you want?" she screamed into the receiver.

"Julie?"

Julie couldn't help laughing. "Oh, Rich, sorry! I'm not exactly a happy camper right now."

"What's up?"

Julie recounted her day: identification of the missing items, meeting with the police chief, the special board meeting.

"The timing just sucks, Rich," Julie concluded. "The meeting won't start until four, and God knows how long it'll last. Under the circumstances, and with what I'll need to do afterwards, I really can't leave until Saturday. Is there any way . . . ?"

"Of course, I'll come!"

"Thanks! Thanks so much," she said.

"No big deal. Is that why you were so wound up when I called?"

"Not really," she said, and described the mysterious telephone calls, both the other night and earlier today.

"It's silly, I know," she said and laughed, "but it's worrisome."

"It isn't silly, and it's more than worrisome. Have you called the police?"

"When you get a new number you get calls to whoever had it before, so I figured that's what was happening."

"But most sane people would ask to speak to the person they were calling," Rich said. "Hang up once, maybe, but not keep at it. I think you should report this right away. Under the circumstances."

"What circumstances?"

"Come on—let's start with the obvious: you're a beautiful young woman living alone in a ski area that's practically deserted. And you're the director of a historical society who just discovered that a bunch of valuable artifacts are missing. Either one is a good reason to call the cops."

"I guess so." She paused. "I want to talk to the police chief about the thefts again tomorrow anyway, when Worth and Howard aren't around, so I'll mention it to him then. You know, instead of calling 9-1-1 and getting a deputy sheriff out here shaking his head over some hysterical woman with an accent."

"Accent?" Rich said. "You don't have an accent."

"I don't have a Maine accent, which means I have an accent. You know what I mean."

"Okay, but please check all those doors and windows, and call me a couple of times tonight, just to check in."

"Sure," she said.

"Caller ID," Rich said abruptly. "You need to get caller ID. Call the phone company first thing in the morning and have them install it right away."

"I can't believe I didn't think of that sooner. I will."

Feeling she was on the way to solving the problem of the phone calls, Julie didn't hesitate to agree to call him every hour until she went to bed.

Rich called at six-fifteen to check on her before his early class. Julie decided to skip a morning walk—not that she was afraid, she told herself—in favor of getting to the office early. Besides, it was already getting warm and sticky. In southern Ohio where she grew up, such a day would have been considered typical of early summer. In Delaware, where she had passed the last four summers, this day would have been welcomed as a touch of fall or spring. But in Ryland, Maine, temperatures already in the low seventies at six-thirty in the morning and predicted to be near ninety by afternoon represented a major heat wave for June. So getting a good start on the workday seemed sensible.

Mrs. Detweiller had not deigned to explain the phone system, but Julie assumed a flashing light meant what it normally did—a message. How to retrieve it was another matter. She found a marginally readable copy of the instruction book in her desk. With its help, she managed to retrieve it: "Ms. Williamson, this is Mike Barlow calling at . . . let's see, it's about nine-fifteen Wednesday evening. You probably won't get this till tomorrow, but please call me anytime in the morning. I'm in early. Thanks."

Was seven-thirty too early? Probably not, and it would demonstrate that, though not a Mainer, she was capable of being at work before noon. Like most others in Ryland, the police chief appeared to favor the abbreviated form of giving a phone number.

"Ryland Police, Chief Barlow," the deep voice said when the phone was picked up after the second ring. Julie identified herself.

"I'm just down the street," Barlow said. "I can be there in a couple of minutes. This a good time?"

Julie welcomed the chance to talk to the policeman in the quiet morning before Mrs. Detweiller and Jason arrived. She told him the coffee would be ready, an offer she hoped she could fulfill by working the ancient coffee machine that sat on the table behind Mrs. Detweiller's desk. No doubt historic, Julie told herself as she filled and started it—at least not missing, she added.

Julie hadn't paid much attention to Chief Michael Barlow when they'd met before, but this morning she took the time to assess him. She liked what she saw: a well-proportioned man in his late thirties, solid but not overweight, about six-foot-two, she guessed, with dark-brown hair cut in short military fashion—handsome, and definitely someone who inspired confidence when called to an emergency. Or, Julie thought, if you were receiving unpleasant phone calls. He wore a khaki uniform with RPD on the sleeve, a bright red badge on his chest, and CHIEF BARLOW stitched in script letters above it.

"Black for me," Barlow replied to Julie's question about how he liked his coffee. He looked up.

"This must be tough for you, starting a new job and finding all these problems."

"I'm still trying to figure out what the problems are," she said. "I mean, are these things all missing? And if so, what happened? It's hard to believe it's a coincidence, but things do get misplaced."

"You think that's what happened—the stuff got misplaced?"

"I really don't know. What do you think?"

"In my business, you learn to think the worst and hope for the best. I'd like to think all this stuff will just turn up, but until it does I have to assume it's been stolen. I put out an alert last night. Right now I'd like to go through this with you and see if we can find any pattern, something to start investigating."

The word got Julie's attention. *Investigating*, she assumed, meant interviewing the staff, asking questions about the missing items. And of course that's what the chief was doing right now, starting with her.

"Now I assume you've never seen any of these items yourself," he continued. "They were gone before you got here, right?"

"Right that I never saw the letters, painting, guns, whatever, but I can't say they were gone before I got here."

"I see what you mean. Tell me about the inventory again."

Julie explained about the missing Lincoln letter, the board discussion, *The Post* article—all points she had touched on the night before, but on which she elaborated now. She also described the inventory system and the way she, Jason, Worth, and Tabby had worked through the cards and verified the existence of the valuable items.

"So you were only looking for valuable stuff," the policeman interrupted. "You didn't do a complete inventory. When I was in high school, I worked at Holdsworth's Hardware, and every January we closed for two days to do inventory. We counted every damned screw and nail, it seems like, and old Clif was there double-checking it."

"So you grew up here?"

"Spent my whole life in Ryland. Except for some time in the army. Anyway, you didn't do the kind of inventory we did at Holdsworth's?"

"No, we really didn't have time for that," Julie said. "Because of the Lincoln letter and the newspaper story, the board wanted to make sure that any valuable items were secure."

"And you defined 'valuable' as you went along."

"I guess that's right. Worth Harding certainly knows the collection, knows what's worth money. And I guess Jason and Tabby do, too, to a lesser degree."

"I see. I'm just trying to make sure I understand. For whatever it's worth, is it fair to say your inventory was selective—that you didn't verify everything?"

"That's right. Are you suggesting there might be other things missing?"

"Just trying to understand. If something's missing at someone's house or a store, I understand how things work, but I don't know much about historical societies. Tell me how artifacts are handled."

Now Julie sensed where the chief was going. "You mean, who handles them, and who might have a chance to take them?" she asked.

Barlow smiled and paused before replying. "Right. I need to identify possible suspects and then see if I can eliminate them."

"Okay, but remember, I'm brand new here."

"That's one of the things that makes you so useful."

Mike pulled out the folder with the pad he had used to take notes the evening before.

"Let's start with Worth Harding," he said.

Julie's discomfort about discussing her predecessor was compounded by her limited knowledge of him, but Mike's professional tone and attitude gave her the confidence to begin.

"Well, he was the director here for years and years, as you know, and he knows a lot more about the procedures and operations than I do."

"I'll be talking to him," Mike said. "Right now I just want your take on things, as a newcomer."

"I should probably close my door," Julie said.

Fifteen

"So the long and short of it," Barlow summarized after Julie described what she knew of how the Ryland Historical Society operated, "is that basically anyone who worked here, or even a volunteer, could have taken any of the items. Is that right?"

"I wouldn't have put it quite that way, but, yes, I guess that's fair," Julie replied.

"Would any of the people we're talking about have a reason to steal any of these items?"

"The Lincoln letter and the muskets are obviously the most valuable, so anyone who wanted money would have a motive for taking them. As for the others, I can't see risking much to get a Klan robe or a bunch of Brigham Young letters, though I'm sure they're worth something."

"How about the painting?"

"I guess that could be valuable enough, but not like the letter and the guns. It seems to me the kind of thing someone might take just because he, or she, liked it."

"You're saying then that Worth, Battles, Tabby Preston, Louise Danners—they might have taken something for money?"

"No more than anyone! I certainly don't mean to say they had any special motive or interest."

"Okay," Mike said with a grin. "I wasn't trying to trip you up. But let's say money is an obvious motive. Do any of the people we've talked about have any special need for it?"

"Who doesn't?"

"But something more than normal?" he prompted.

Julie paused before answering. What Worth had said to her about Jason's expensive lifestyle was only hearsay, after all. Well, no, she admitted to herself. She was aware of his expensive car.

"You're thinking of something," Mike observed. "Look, let me make clear again that I'm just poking around here to get a picture. I'm going to talk to all these people myself, but because you're new here, you can provide a different perspective. And nothing you tell me goes any further."

Julie described her conversation with Worth about Jason, emphasizing that she was only repeating what she had been told.

"Ever see his car?" Mike asked.

Julie admitted that she had, but pretended not to see the significance of it.

"In a small town, cops know everyone's car after a while—by sight and even many by just the sound," Mike continued. "A

Beemer like his isn't common around here, at least not year-round."

Mike made a few notes on his pad and then looked up.

"I can see you're thinking of something else," he said.

"The painting. Jason was an art history major in college. I don't know if that's significant."

"Not sure there's a statute in Maine against art history majors, but I'll make a note that he might have some interest in paintings."

Julie laughed and waited for him to resume.

"How about Worth—you think he needs money?"

"He's donating his house to the Society," Julie said. "If he needed money, wouldn't he just sell it?"

"Suppose so. Or the two muskets he owned himself. How about Tabitha Preston?"

"I don't really know her."

"Any of the others—Louise Danners, other volunteers?"

"Again, I just can't say. But you seem to be concentrating on the people here. What about outside thieves—like in the newspaper story?"

"I'm not forgetting them, but there's nothing I can do on that front until I get some response to the stolen-items alert. In the meantime, I need to check on inside possibilities. You've been very helpful. I'll keep you informed. And when you get those valuations for Henry LaBelle, pleave give me a copy."

He handed her his card.

"Fax number's on there, or drop it off at the station. Now I'd like to talk to the others, and unless you mind, I'd like to start with your secretary."

"Mrs. Detweiller must be in by now," Julie said and looked at her watch. It was almost nine-thirty. "One question before you go, though. I've been trying to decide what to tell people here about the missing items, and when. Shouldn't I say something before you start asking questions?"

"Your call. Why don't we start with your secretary? You can call her in and tell her I'm looking into the disappearance of some items, and then while I interview her you can go around and talk to the others. Make sense?"

Julie went to the door and asked Mrs. Detweiller to come in. After describing the situation, she left the secretary and policeman in her office while she headed to Jason's; she then made the rounds of the three Society buildings to inform everyone else. It wasn't as neat and clean as she would have liked, but within a half-hour she had finished the job. When she returned to the office Mrs. Detweiller was at her desk.

"The chief's with Jason," Mrs. Detweiller said. "What a terrible situation! This sort of thing never happened at the Society before."

Before I arrived, Julie translated to herself.

"We don't really know what's happened, Mrs. Detweiller. We just need to be sure about these items, and Chief Barlow has to ask questions. I hope this information won't go beyond us here."

"Well, *The Gazette* doesn't come out till Tuesday, so that should help."

"*Gazette?*" Julie asked.

"Our town paper—*The Ryland Gazette*—it comes out on Tuesday. So the news won't get out till then. But everyone will know after Tuesday."

Julie noted that Mrs. Detweiller conveniently failed to pledge her own confidence on the point, but she didn't want to make too much of it.

"I see," was the only response she made.

She started to go back to her office but stopped. "When the chief's finished with Jason, could you ask him to come to my office, please?"

"The chief?"

"No, Jason."

"I'll ask," Mrs. Detweiller said, emphasizing the verb, as if the outcome of such a foolish request was not something she would want to take personal responsibility for.

"Thank you, Mrs. Detweiller," Julie said crisply. "In the meantime, where would I find the files on the Society's insurance policies?"

Last night's quick review of the insurance file hadn't been very helpful, but Julie thought a little more time might yield something. It didn't, but while she was reviewing the folder Mrs. Detweiller came to the door to say Henry LaBelle was on the phone. And Jason was free to see her.

"Ask Jason to wait while I take this call. And could you close the door, please?"

"Sorry to hear about this," Henry began. "Howard left a message for me last night, and I talked to him this morning. Sounds like we need to process a claim."

Julie happily noted he had used the plural pronoun. "Now what do we know about values?" the trustee-lawyer-insurance agent continued.

"Well, as we discussed at the board meeting, we don't have specific appraisals. I did make a call about the Lincoln letter, and an expert told me probably $20,000 to $25,000. It could be more or less, of course. Do I need to give you exact figures?"

"I just need a range—we'll worry about specifics later. The point of the range is to let the carrier know the rough damage—a sort of heads-up."

"Okay," Julie said, "the biggest items are the muskets. I'd say at least $100,000 each, possibly more."

"Now the painting, the other letters, the Klan stuff. What do you think about them?"

"I'd say at least $5,000, maybe more, for the painting. The Brigham Young letters might be another $5,000, and maybe the Klan outfit would be $1,000. But I'm only guessing. I can start doing some real work on this."

"Let's hope that's not necessary. Mike Barlow said he put out an alert. Maybe everything will turn up. But for now, let's call it a quarter- to a half-million total. That sound about right?"

"That sounds obscene," Julie answered. "I mean, it's probably a good overall estimate, but it really sounds awful. A half-million dollars! Would we be covered on all that?"

"I think so, but I need to do some checking, too. I don't think we scheduled any property, but there's an umbrella here. I need to make a few calls. Can I get back to you later?"

Julie told Henry she would be at the Society all day. And probably all weekend, she added to herself after the call ended. It wasn't what she had planned. Nor was dealing with a theft of maybe a half-million dollars!

When she walked out to Mrs. Detweiller's desk on her way to invite Jason to her office, Julie saw Chief Barlow sitting in a chair by the file cabinets, working on his notes.

"Wondered if you'd settled the values," Mike explained.

"I just talked to Henry LaBelle," she replied. "Do you want to come in?"

"That much?" Mike said after Julie had told him the sum.

"Only a rough estimate," she said. "Henry said that's all he needed right now."

"I can use that," the policeman said, and made a note. "I'd better go along and talk to the others."

"There's just one more thing, if you have a minute."

She told him about the phone calls. He was silent for a few moments, the only sound the tapping of his pen on his legal pad.

"You think there's a connection?" he asked.

"With the thefts? I don't see how, but I thought I should mention the calls."

"Can you think of anyone who might be doing it? Could there be someone who might want to give you a hard time?"

"No."

"A man? Old boyfriends can sometimes be a problem."

"I don't have an old boyfriend. My longtime and current one teaches at UMaine, but there's no problem there."

"Sorry to ask, but would you mind giving me his name and phone number? Just for the record." He wrote Rich's name and number on his pad. "I guess you don't have caller ID?"

"No, but I'm planning to get it."

"The phone company will say so. Of course, they make money that way." He laughed. "Although they might put it on for a short time for free. I'd call them right away. Do you feel safe up there on the mountain by yourself?"

"I did, but maybe I shouldn't."

"I'm not saying that. Why don't I come up and have a look around? Check things out? Okay if I come up later today?"

They agreed on six p.m. When he left, she called the phone company to report the calls. For $15 a month she ordered caller ID, to be installed immediately. It would be a week before she'd get the readout box—this was rural Maine, after all—but in the meantime, the telephone company would be able to monitor her calls.

Sixteen

After she'd finished her meeting with Chief Barlow and called the phone company, Julie remembered she had asked to see Jason. Things just seemed to keep slipping, and Julie knew herself well enough to understand that she was rarely at her best unless she was in control.

"Sorry to keep you waiting," she said when he came into her office.

"Plenty to do," he said. "Anything I can do to help?"

Where to begin? Julie wondered as she thought of the several reasons she had wanted to see him. Before she could answer, he said: "It's worse in the afternoon. Because you face west."

Julie stared at him, wondering what in the world he was talking about.

"I'm sorry," Jason said, recognizing her confusion. "It's hot in here, and I was just saying that your office gets worse in the afternoon because it faces west. On hot days, Worth used to work at home in the afternoon. But maybe you're more used to weather like this."

Julie realized that she *was* hot, that sweat was running down her arms and off her neck.

"Maybe I should open the rest of the windows," she said.

"I'll do it."

He jumped up and moved around her desk and began opening the three windows that faced the Common.

"These are tricky, by the way—you have to prop them open with one of these sticks." He picked up a two-foot length of thin board and placed it in the windowsill.

"I wondered what they were for," Julie said. "Thanks."

Jason proceeded to open and prop the other two windows. When he finished, he came back around the desk and stood a few feet from where she had been standing as she watched him work. "One of the problems with old buildings," he said. "You have to know all the tricks."

She used the time he had worked on the windows to decide how to begin.

"I wish we could have had this talk earlier. I meant to, but you know how busy it's gotten, and with so many unexpected things . . ."

"The thefts," Jason prompted.

"Or whatever. It wasn't exactly how I'd hoped to begin this job. But, anyway, what I wanted to talk about was you—your job, what you plan to do, how you see things here, how we can work together."

"That's a big topic, but of course I'm happy to talk about myself," Jason said with a chuckle.

"Unfortunately," Julie interjected quickly, "the time still isn't right for that kind of conversation. Right now I need to focus on these missing items. That's really what I'd like to talk to you about now."

"Barlow already grilled me," Jason said. "I don't think I'm a suspect, but maybe you should ask him that."

"I'm not saying that. But two of the missing items involve you, and I'm concerned about good museum practice."

He started to speak again, but she put up her hand to stop him. "Let me finish. First the painting—you should have been aware that the volunteers had substituted one. I know volunteers aren't perfect, but we really depend on them, and they need to inform you about things like that, or you need to pay attention yourself."

"You're right, but most of the volunteers look to Worth as their boss. I'm just a kid in their minds. I'm surprised they didn't tell Worth, but I accept the fact that I should have picked up on the switch myself."

"We can work out a process with the volunteers so they know to report things to you. But then there's the Brigham Young correspondence. You know that letters like that shouldn't leave the library. It's just not good museum practice, whatever your intention."

"My intention was simple. I wanted to verify the quotations, and the easiest way was to look at them while I had the text of my notes on the screen in front of me. Wrong? Sure, I admit that. But I was trying to be careful." He paused and looked down at his lap for a few seconds before resuming. "Look, do you want to fire me? Just say so if you do. You don't have to beat around the bush. I knew that a new director might want to make changes."

"No, Jason, I don't want to fire you. I just want to be sure we understand each other. I have high standards about how this place should run. I think you do, too. And I want to be sure we agree, that—"

A knock on the door cut Julie off in mid-sentence.

"Call for you, Dr. Williamson," Mrs. Detweiller said after Julie had opened the door. "The phone company—about your 'calling identity.' "

Jason half-rose to indicate his willingness to leave. Julie gestured for him to stay. "Sorry. This shouldn't take long."

"Yes," she said into the phone. "That's correct. Yes. Caller ID. Yes, I understand the fee. Right away. Thank you."

Jason stood up as soon as she hung up the phone. "Consider my hand slapped."

"All I want is for you to understand that you made a couple of mistakes and that you won't repeat them. Clear the air and move on."

"I blew it on the painting and I blew it on the Young letters. What else do you want me to do?"

This just wasn't the interview Julie had hoped to have. She blamed herself—the timing was wrong, the circumstances just didn't work. She decided to cut her losses.

"I think that's all, Jason. Let's just leave it here for now. Next week, when we get this behind us, I really do want to talk about all the other things. Let's set a time now to be sure."

They settled on a two-hour block of time toward the end of the following week. Jason went into his office. The whole meeting hadn't been what she had wanted, but at least she had done it. She couldn't second-guess herself now.

Seventeen

"See you've learned to use natural air-conditioning," Mike Barlow said to her when Julie walked him into the living room at precisely six o'clock that evening. "Close against the sun, open for the dark, that's what we do around here in a heat wave," he continued. "But I suppose under the circumstances you might not want to reopen later. Can I just check around a bit?"

Julie led him through the condo and watched as he carefully examined the windows and doors.

"I really appreciate your driving all the way out here for this," Julie said.

"That's my job," he said. "You did take care of caller ID?"

"Right after you left."

"Great. Did you mention to anyone that you were having it installed—anyone at the historical society?"

"No, I made the call myself."

"Good. If the person who's making these calls finds out you're getting ID, they might start to use an ID block to keep their names from showing, or they might stop calling. So if someone knew, and then the calls stopped, we'd have a clue."

"Wait a minute! I just remembered: the phone company called back and Mrs. Detweiller took the call. She knows, and then she told me about it in front of Jason."

"Interesting. Let's see what happens. If the calls do stop, that might tell us something."

"Jason? Why would he be calling me?"

"Didn't say he was. We'll just see what happens," he repeated. "Could I trouble you for something to drink?"

"Of course, what would you like?"

"Iced tea? Anything soft."

"Venus," the policeman said when she came into the living room with the tea.

"Venus?" she repeated.

"That goes right here," he said, and pointed to a missing section of the solar system puzzle on the coffee table.

Julie laughed. "Oh, thanks. I'm afraid I've been neglecting that. Are you a puzzle person?"

Now it was Mike's turn to laugh. "Isn't that what cops do?"

"I guess so. I always say that's why I became a historian—because I like to solve puzzles."

They walked out to the deck.

"You must like the weather here, being a native," Julie said as they took in the view.

"It suits me. I did my basic training in Virginia and figured that was as hot as it could get, but then they sent me to Georgia for MP school. That was just too much. So I was happy to come home."

"When was that?"

"Long time ago—eleven, twelve years, I guess."

"To be police chief?"

"Not right away. Went to the state police academy in Waterville and started on the force, and became chief three years ago."

"It must be nice living where you grew up."

"Like I said, Ryland suits me."

"It's easy to see why. I just love it here. It's such a gorgeous area."

"Weather could use some improving, though," he said. "Not many people around here like this heat."

Julie had been in Ryland long enough to realize that weather was not just a general topic of conversation, a way to open a chat or fill an awkward silence. No, in Ryland weather was a staple item, maybe even bordering on an obsession: it was too hot, or too cold, or it would become one or the other if you just waited long enough. She felt obliged to contribute to the topic.

"But this is unusually hot, right?"

"Yeah, it should break in a few days. And then we'll go back to complaining about it not being warm enough," he said with a smile. "Not much else to talk about in a small town like this."

"Did you ever want to live somewhere bigger?"

"Thought about it, especially after the army, but high school girlfriend—the usual story," he said, and laughed.

Julie glanced at the policeman's left hand: no wedding ring. He noticed her look and said, "Divorced. High school sweethearts don't necessarily last long in marriages.

"So you feel pretty safe here?" he asked abruptly, changing the subject.

"I did," Julie answered, feeling awkward about having been so personal. "But the calls spooked me, I have to admit. If they do stop now, would you suspect Jason?"

"I'd want to talk with him. Is there any reason he might have been making those calls, anything you sensed about him?"

"I really haven't figured him out yet. The first couple of times we talked, I sort of felt like he was being overly friendly, maybe even flirting, but that hasn't happened since. And today he was sarcastic and angry when I talked to him about being careless with the Brigham Young letters and the painting. I think he's just young."

"Well, he's that," the chief said. "By the way, you need to change the security code on the historical society buildings. I have a sense that Worth Harding never thought about things like that."

"I know, I just haven't gotten around to it. I'll do it first thing in the morning."

"Good. And give the new code only to those who absolutely need it. Who would that be?"

"Well, Jason primarily. He opens and closes the place. Maybe some of the volunteers would need it, but I'll limit it to the smallest number of people possible."

Julie jumped as Mike's beeper went off. He reached down to read the number. "Have to run," he explained. "One problem with a heat wave is that it encourages people to do dumb things, and it looks like someone has. Probably some good old boys having too many brews. Thanks again. And don't forget Venus."

She had to think for a second but then remembered and laughed.

Mike left quickly, and Julie watched him as he got into his car and spoke on the radio before driving off quickly. While he hadn't done anything except look over her apartment and check windows and doors, his visit had comforted her. Good to know there was a helpful police chief nearby. And, interesting to find out more about him: the small-town kid who went off to the army and came back to marry his high school girlfriend—and then got divorced. He seemed like a great guy, hard to imagine someone not wanting to stay married to him. Go figure, Julie said to herself just as her phone rang. She let the answering machine pick up and as soon as she heard Rich's voice, she picked up the receiver.

"Sorry, Rich. Just let the message finish."

When it did, he said, "Glad you're not answering. Any more calls?"

"Not since I've been home, and the police chief was here with me."

She described her conversation in the morning with Mike, how she was getting caller ID, her meeting with Jason, and Mike's suggestion she should be on her guard around him.

"Interesting," Rich said.

"Rich, you sound like Mike Barlow. He seems to find 'interesting' an interesting word, too."

"Well it is interesting, and the cop's right—if your calls stop, Battles will look like a pretty good suspect since he knows you got caller ID."

"I'm not as worried about the calls as I am about the thefts. And you'll be here tomorrow, right?"

He confirmed the plan, and they agreed he would call again later on and that she would let all calls roll to the answering machine. His call at eleven was the only other one of the evening. "So maybe the cop's right," Rich said when she told him that. "Maybe it was Battles and he'll stop now because you can trace him."

"Or maybe the jerk just got tired of it," Julie said. "In any case, I can't wait to see you tomorrow. Drive safely."

"You be safe, too."

Eighteen

When she woke at five-thirty, Julie realized it had been the soundest sleep she had had in several nights—despite the heat. And she could tell already it was going to be another hot day. She went immediately to the office to work in its relative coolness until she felt it was not too early to call New York.

"Even up there?" Maurice Leary said after Julie had begun her phone conversation with news of the oppressive heat. "I thought Maine was cool in the summer."

"So did I, Maurice, but believe me, the heat here is as bad as in Delaware or New York right now."

"But whereas I'm sitting in my air-conditioned office at the auction house right now, you're praying for a fan."

"That's exactly right—nothing's air-conditioned here except my car. I'm tempted to move into it. But I don't mean to keep you, Maurice. Is this a good time to talk?"

"About a letter from A. Lincoln to Hannibal Hamlin?" he asked.

"That. And more. Do you have five minutes?"

"I'll start the timer," he kidded. Ten minutes later, they were still talking.

"Sounds like you've gotten into something rather strange up there," Leary said. "I'll need to do some checking, but I'd guess a half-million is about right. I did have a chance to work a little on the Lincoln item, and I think my original guess holds—$20,000 to $25,000. Remember I mentioned we had an autograph sale last summer? We sold one for $15,000, but it wasn't to anyone as well known as Hamlin. Anyway, the big-ticket items are the muskets. We just sold one here for $235,000. If yours are similar, the two of them ought to fetch a half-million. I suppose the Maine connection—the fact the muskets were used on the Arnold expedition to Quebec—might raise that a bit for a local collector. The painting won't bring much unless it's signed. The Klan stuff is negligible.

"The Brigham Young correspondence is hard to value because the Mormons, as you know, are major collectors with deep pockets," he continued. "If we put up some Young letters, we'd know the church would go for them and would have the resources to get them. In a bidding war, they could fetch a good price. The LDS can buy what it wants."

"LDS?" Julie asked.

"Church of Jesus Christ of Latter-day Saints—the Mormons."

"Oh, right."

"Anyway, let me do a little checking here and get back to you on some values. I'll call you later this morning."

Julie was delighted her old mentor had offered to help. With the resources of the auction house, he'd be able to get good estimates faster than she could. And, coming from him, the numbers would be credible. Now she'd take care of the security code.

"We've sent several reminders about this," the woman at the security company said. "We do recommend changing the code periodically. We'll send someone out to do the work, and at that time they will need to have a written authorization from you," the woman continued, "as well as some official confirmation that you're authorized to change and use the code. Meantime, I can work on a new one for you. Do you have any preference about the numbers—something you can remember easily is best, but I'd recommend staying away from the obvious. Your old code starts with 7-4-7. People could easily guess it."

"They could?"

"Think about the telephone pad—with letters for each number. 7-4-7 is RHS. Ryland Historical Society. And the rest of the code is 1-8-0-2. That's the year that Ryland was settled. So your current code is 7-4-7-1-8-0-2. Ryland Historical Society and 1802. What would you like?"

Julie had an idea, a code no one around Ryland would think of.

"I'll run this through the computer and make sure it's available. We'll have someone out there Monday. You can fill out the forms then about who else is authorized to use the code."

"Of course. Thanks so much."

RHS-1802, Julie thought. The woman was right—it wouldn't take much to guess that. On the other hand, who would want to try? A thief, she answered herself. But what if the thief already had access to the code because he worked at the Ryland Historical Society?

As she was contemplating that prospect, some other letters strayed into her mind—LDS. When they had looked for the

Brigham Young letters, they had, of course, checked the "Y" box, along with the ones immediately before and after it. They had also checked the "M" box for Mormon. But they hadn't checked "L," for LDS. It was a thin possibility, but it was worth checking. Julie would love to remove at least one set of items from the missing list she was going to discuss with the board this afternoon.

The library was empty when she climbed the stairs and opened the door to enter it. On such a hot day, how could Tabitha Preston stand to work up here? But Julie had seen her earlier coming in to take her accustomed place in the library. Tabby wasn't at her desk now. Probably gone for a drink of water, Julie decided, since she was sure Tabby would never contemplate bringing such a dangerous substance as water to her desk, even on such a blazing hot day.

Julie was surprised to see the vault door open. The heat must surely be getting the better of poor Tabby if she left the vault open when she stepped out. Making sure the door was wide open, Julie entered the vault and located the "L" box. Before she could even turn back around, the vault door slammed shut. Her first thought was the wind, but then she realized that this boiling day was without wind. Someone had closed the door to the vault! Surely not deliberately, she thought. Probably Tabby returned, saw the door open and moved quickly to cover up her little mistake. But if she was back in the library, why would she close the vault?

Julie's thoughts came fast, not because it mattered what had happened, but because she was doing whatever she could to keep from thinking about the obvious—she was locked in a vault. Stay calm, she told herself. This isn't really a problem. I'll just yell. Tabby will hear me and open the door.

She started at a low, conversational level, calling out, "Tabby? Tabby? Are you there? I'm in the vault. Will you please open it."

Then she said it a little louder.

Then, as the walls started to close in, she really screamed.

"Help! Help me! I'm locked in the vault. *Open this door!*"

She beat her fists on the door as she screamed, each blow heavier than the one before, tracking in its intensity the rising panic of her voice.

"Please, please! Open this door."

Sweat poured off her. She realized it was dripping onto the "L" box on the floor. Poor museum practice, she scolded herself out loud, hoping a sense of perspective would help settle her. Thinking about sweat running onto historical documents seemed appropriately insane under the circumstances, and that fact oddly cheered her. She thought she heard movement outside the door and resumed her call, but the door remained tightly closed. And the more she thought of that, the deeper her panic became. She couldn't resist saying to herself the very words she knew she should avoid:

Closed door.

Airtight seal.

No escape.

Geting tighter.

I'm going to die.

She began to shake as she pounded furiously against the door. And then, just as she wound up to give the door one more serious blow, it swung open. She threw herself into the arms of Jason Battles.

"Thank God!" she screamed.

"Are you okay?" Jason asked when she had disengaged herself. "What happened?"

"I went in to check something, and the door closed. I screamed and beat on the door. I'm claustrophobic and, God, I've got to sit down. I feel sick."

Jason helped her to a chair and crouched down beside her. "Let me get you some water."

"No, please. Just stay here. I'll be okay in a minute."

"You really need some water."

"No, please, don't leave me here," Julie said.

It was the last thing she said before she passed out.

Nineteen

Mrs. Detweiller and Tabitha Preston were standing above her. She could also make out Jason's face. She heard words being exchanged, but she couldn't understand what was said.

Jason took her shoulders and gently lifted them from the floor. Julie pulled her legs up and got into a sitting position.

"I think I'd like that water now, Jason," she said.

"It's right here," he said, handing her a paper cup.

"Thank you. And thank you for letting me out."

"How did you get locked in there? I just came into the library and saw Tabby was gone, and I was going to go back downstairs when I thought I heard something."

"The vault was open when I got here," Julie began, "and I went in . . ."

"That's impossible," Tabby sharply interjected. "I was taking my break and I always lock the vault when I leave the room. It's standard procedure. You know that, Jason."

"It was open, Tabby," Julie said. "I'm sorry, but it was."

Tabby scowled.

"I've never failed to follow procedures. It was stuffy in here so I went down to get a drink. I closed the vault and locked it when I left. If you don't believe me, then—"

"Of course I believe you," Julie interrupted quickly. "But you need to believe me when I say the vault was open. We'll clear this up, don't worry." Although she didn't necessarily believe herself, Julie felt stronger now and rose from the chair.

"Be careful," Jason said. "You're still weak."

But Julie was determined.

"I went into the vault to check something, and I want to finish that. You see, I had this idea that maybe the Brigham Young correspondence was here."

She leaned over and lifted the L box that was just inside the vault. Even though Jason, Tabby and Mrs. Detweiller were all there, she was reluctant to step too far into the vault. She carried the box to the table. Small drops of water, the result of her sweat, were visible across the tops of the folders.

"Do you have a paper towel, Tabby? I'm afraid I was sweating badly in there and some of it dripped onto these folders."

Tabitha Preston found some paper towels on her desk and Julie carefully wiped the tops of the folders.

"No harm done," she said. "Now, let me just look."

The others stood by in silence as Julie worked through the folders. "Yes!" she exclaimed. "It's here—the Young folder!"

She pulled out the folder and held it triumphantly before her.

"Misfiled," Tabby said. "I don't understand that."

"Not misfiled," Julie said. "Just filed under a letter we hadn't thought about. Mormons are also called LDS, for Latter-day Saints. We checked Mormon and Young before, but we didn't check LDS."

"How could I forget?" Jason said. "Of course—I returned those letters just like I said, but I put them in the 'L' box. I remember now."

Julie watched Jason closely as he spoke but couldn't detect anything more than pleasure on his face. And no wonder—he was off the hook now, the letters safe.

"I'm afraid this is all beyond me," Mrs. Detweiller said, her first words in many minutes. "I'd better leave you all to this and get back downstairs. I'll be in my office."

"Well, that's cleared up then," Tabby said. "But I still don't understand about the vault. I closed and locked it. There's just no explanation for why it was open."

"The important thing is that the letters are here," Jason said. "Now you can take them off the list of missing items."

"Exactly," Julie said. "That's one mystery solved. Wish the other items would reappear so easily."

"Maybe they will," Jason said.

"Don't worry about all this, Tabby," Julie said. I'm sure you followed procedures. It doesn't matter now."

"That's right," Jason said, looking at Tabby. "You shouldn't worry. I need to get over to Holder House. I've got a tour. Do you need me for anything else, Julie?"

"No, but thanks again for getting me out of there. I'm sure the wind blew the door shut; I was just lucky you came by."

Wind, Julie thought as she walked into her office. What wind? The air was perfectly still. But she'd had to say something to end the conversation in the library. She needed time to think about what had happened, but right now she needed to prepare her notes for the afternoon board meeting. She looked forward to reporting that at least one of the items had been found; whether she would explain the circumstances of finding the letters, she was not so sure.

"This is a sad occasion for the Ryland Historical Society," Howard Townsend intoned somberly after calling the meeting to order. Howard had phoned Julie at two to suggest that she not arrange the usual cookies and coffee. "Not quite right for the occasion," he had told her. The trustees seemed to understand that today was a different sort of meeting because they assembled in full just before four and immediately took their seats at the table. The banter and private conversations Julie had observed at the Monday meeting were not in evidence today.

"You're all aware," Howard continued, "that we have experienced some unpleasantness. I called this special meeting to discuss what has happened. Henry, under the circumstances, may we dispense with the reading of the minutes from Monday's meeting?"

"Since they're not written up yet, I think that's highly appropriate, Howard," Henry answered. "I'll note that we dispensed with the reading of the minutes because this is a special session."

"Is that really kosher?" Clif Holdsworth asked. "We need to be on the up-and-up here."

"It's perfectly okay, Clif," Henry said.

"If you say so," Clif said, though his tone suggested that he harbored his own doubts.

"Then let's go directly to our business," Howard said. "I'm sure everyone remembers that we directed Julie to undertake a complete inventory of our holdings."

"Not complete," Worth Harding pointed out. "We instructed her to check on items we considered valuable."

"I stand corrected," Howard said. "An inventory of valuable items. And the results of that were not pleasing. I've tried to bring you all up to date on the situation, but I'd like to call on our director to make her report now. As she'll explain, we have five items—actually more than five items, but let's say five groups of items—that have been identified as missing. Julie, please go ahead."

When Julie had taken Howard's phone call at two, she had started to tell him that there was recent news, but he'd cut her off quickly, saying he wanted to hear everything at the same time the other trustees did. Although his lack of curiosity surprised her, she explained it to herself as a consequence of his fussy ways.

"Four items now," she began. "Or groups, as Howard says. One item was found just this morning."

Julie described the search, crediting Worth, Jason, and Tabby for their long hours of work. She then listed the missing items, including the Brigham Young correspondence.

"This morning, however," she said, "we located the Young letters. They had been filed in the 'L' box rather than 'Y' for Young or 'M' for Mormon."

"That seems peculiar," Martha Preston interrupted. "The library is very carefully organized and run. I think we all know how professionally my sister performs her job there. Why would these letters be in the 'L' box?"

Julie explained, and noted that Jason remembered returning the letters to the "L" box. She really didn't want to get into the question of why he had taken them out in the first place, but Martha was not going to allow her to skirt the issue.

"But that's simply not good practice," she said after Julie explained how Jason had removed the letters from the library. "Materials of any kind must remain in the library at all times. That's standard practice, everyone knows that. Not that we'd expect someone like Worth to know."

"The important thing is that the letters are secure."

"Unlike the guns, the painting, the Klan robe, and our old friend the Lincoln letter," Dalton Scott said. "Let's focus on those."

Although Dalton's question was directed at the chairman and he was looking in his direction as he spoke, Martha apparently considered herself the target. "Ignoring good practices is what got us into this in the first place, Mr. Scott. But if you want us to just go blithely on, overlooking the tragic errors in the matter of the Young letters, well, I'm not about to be a martyr."

"I can't see how it makes you a martyr, dear," Mary Ellen Swanson said, "but if you have more to say about this, I'd like to hear it."

Obviously pleased with what she regarded as the endorsement of another trustee, Martha continued: "My only point, Mary Ellen, is that if sloppy practices were in place in one area, they may have been in others. So perhaps the other items listed will also be found. If we can understand what happened to the Brigham Young letters, then perhaps we can locate the guns, the painting, and the Lincoln letter."

"And the Klan outfit," Mary Ellen added. "Perhaps it was just misfiled, too. That's really what you're saying, isn't it, Martha?"

"I doubt that," Worth said. "I haven't had the chance to talk to Julie about how she found the Young letters, but it's unlikely the other missing items will magically reappear in surprise places. I agree with Dalton—let's focus on the missing items, not the found ones."

"That's fine," Martha said tensely, leaned back in her chair, and folded her arms across her chest as if to say that the group would simply have to get along without her good sense.

"What's the damage?" Loretta Cummings asked.

"Well, of course there's the damage to our reputation—the Society, the board, even the town itself," Howard answered. "And then . . ."

"No," Cummings said, "I mean the value—how much money are we talking about here?"

"Somewhere between a half- and three-quarters of a million dollars," Julie said.

"Not counting the Young correspondence?" Loretta asked.

"Right. The muskets are the big items, and of course I'm not counting Worth's, just the two the Society owns."

"Well, that gets my attention," Loretta said. "Are we insured for all this, Henry?"

"I'd like to say we are," the lawyer replied, "but I haven't been able to get a definitive answer from the carrier yet. With big-ticket items, they like to have separate schedules, which we didn't do, but I think I can use some influence with them to cover everything under the umbrella. Our total is $4 million, but that covers buildings as well as contents. We're going to have to work this out. But remember, folks—the thefts have been reported, and there's a chance we'll recover some of the items."

"Where does that stand, Julie?" Dalton asked.

"Chief Barlow put out an alert, and he's been in to talk to the staff. I think we've done everything we can on that front."

"Talk to the staff?" Mary Ellen asked. "May I ask his purpose?"

"To complete his report," Julie answered carefully. "I assume he needs to interview people about when they saw the items and things like that."

"Are staff members under suspicion?"

"Not that I know of," Julie said, knowing that the conversation she had had with Mike about Jason wasn't a matter she should make public. "I'm sure it's routine."

"Mike's very thorough," Dalton said. "He'll do exactly what needs to be done. In the meantime, I don't think we should be discussing suspects. We need to concentrate on what we can do to help Julie. For example, should we have a public statement on this? *The Gazette* will be out on Tuesday, and it's hard to believe they won't pick up on this from someone."

"The Society's reputation is a precious asset," the chairman said. "I agree we need to protect it. Loretta, I know you have to deal with the press all the time about school issues. I wonder if we might impose on you to work with Julie on a statement we could issue."

"I'm no expert on media relations," the school principal said, "but I'll help in any way I can. Maybe Julie and I can get together for a few minutes after the meeting and put something together. Henry ought to look at it, too, don't you think?"

"I think that's very wise," Howard said. "So let's consider that matter taken care of. Thank you for offering your help, Loretta. Now, Julie, what other matters do we need to consider here?"

Glancing at her watch, Julie saw it was nearly five. She knew from Monday's meeting that Howard liked to limit board meetings to an hour.

"I can't think of anything right now," she said. "Our main purpose was to bring everyone up to date, and I think we've done that. If anyone has questions, I'll be happy to try to answer them."

"I do," Martha said. "But then I've already been told to mind my own business."

"Now, Martha, no one told you that," Howard said. "As a member of this board you have every right to ask any question you like."

"I'm troubled about why the Society's muskets from Benedict Arnold's Quebec expedition were at Worth's house," she said. She did not bother to phrase her concern as a question nor did she acknowledge Worth's presence. "It seems Worth did what he wanted, regardless of how it affected the Society."

Julie noted that several of the others looked down at the table rather than make eye contact with the former director.

"I thought they would be safe there," Worth said. "I keep lots of valuable things there, as most of you know."

He glanced at Martha, but Julie couldn't see the woman's response. Then he laughed a little uneasily, that high-pitched laugh she had come to identify with him.

"I was obviously wrong," Worth continued, "and I'm truly sorry for that. Most of you know I rarely lock my doors—who in Ryland does? But the cabinet they were in was locked, I'm sure of that. So who got in and when—well, I just don't know. And I don't know what else I can say. Or do."

It amazed Julie to think Worth would be so careless, but as she scanned the faces around the table, she noticed no one seemed surprised.

"You shouldn't concern yourself, Worth," Howard said. "You did the right thing—took extra precautions. I think the board owes you our thanks for that. You couldn't have known what would happen. I daresay, you've suffered quite a loss yourself. Martha, I think we can agree that Worth did the right thing, and the loss is just that—a loss. Now, I'm sure you're all ready to get home to supper, so I'll entertain a motion to adjourn."

Twenty

"I think Martha's right," Loretta said to Julie as they walked to Swanson House after the meeting. "Worth storing museum property in his house, Jason keeping valuable letters out of the vault—that kind of thing needs to be looked into and corrected."

"I've spoken to Jason, and I'm going to do a solid training program on collection-management procedures for everyone when we get this behind us."

"Good! That's just what this place needs. That's why I agree with Martha, though her timing wasn't the greatest. And she just can't resist taking a swing at Worth when she gets the chance."

"I noticed that," Julie replied. "He seems to ignore her."

"I think that's what gets to her—he eggs her on that way. It's a funny relationship," she said. "Wasn't Howard amazing—adjourning the meeting like that after singing Worth's praises? He's the only one I know who can silence Martha."

"I haven't gotten to know Martha yet," Julie said. "Hate to sound like a broken record, but lots of the things I planned to do in the first couple of weeks have gotten buried by these thefts. I really do need to talk to her about the shop. Of course I've had some chance to work with her sister, and if they're similar I guess I know what to expect."

"Similar? I guess they are. While they're terribly competitive between themselves, they both do good work for the Society."

Despite her modest assertion at the board meeting, Loretta, Julie quickly learned, knew a good deal about what to say and how to say it in a press release. It took them only fifteen minutes to draft and revise a simple statement.

"After you run this by Henry, you can drop it off at the newspaper office and that should take care of things," Loretta said. "They'll probably call and ask for more details, but just play it cool and stick to what we wrote. Now I hope you can at least enjoy your weekend. Do you feel you've gotten settled into Ryland yet?"

"My boyfriend came last weekend, and we did some hiking. He's coming again tonight, so I hope we can get out some more and see the area. It's really lovely."

"It certainly is—that's the main reason most of us stay here. Is your boyfriend from around here?"

Julie explained.

"I hope I'll have a chance to meet him sometime. When all this gets settled, I'll arrange a party some weekend when he's here so you can meet more people."

"That would be great."

Loretta stood to leave, but Julie decided to take one more stab at getting some information.

"Loretta," she said, "can I just ask one more thing? What you said about Worth and Martha having a funny relationship?"

"Martha and Worth were an item before she moved away. When she came back she wanted to pick up where they left off. But . . . well, who knows?"

"That might explain why they seem to go at each other during the meetings."

"Well, it could—that and just orneriness! Both of them have enough of that."

After Loretta left, Julie faxed the draft to Henry with a cover sheet asking him to call her at home over the weekend with comments. She hoped to get it approved so she could drop it off at the newspaper over the weekend and then put the Ryland Historical Society on hold long enough to enjoy Rich's visit.

He was early. When she heard the knock at the door only a few minutes after she arrived home at six, she jumped because she hadn't expected him until seven. Traffic was light, he told her. "Besides, I was worried about you; I wanted to get here as fast as I could."

They had no sooner retreated to the deck, when Rich said, "Your turn."

"Mine's going to take a while," Julie said. "Let's start with you."

It wasn't until they were halfway through dinner that Julie's turn came, and she started with the vault.

"That's awful," Rich said, and stood up to come over and embrace her.

"It really was—you know how claustrophobic I am."

"Did you report it?"

"To the police? No. Besides, I told the chief about the phone calls, and I don't want to come off like a silly girl."

"You're not a silly girl—you're a victim. You've got to report this."

"In the morning, maybe. I just want to think about it more. It just doesn't add up—too many little pieces that don't fit."

"But in the capable hands of our puzzle-master . . ." Rich said to prompt her. He sat silently as Julie told him the whole story.

"Interesting," he said when she finished. "Let's start with the library volunteer—do you believe her?"

"That she closed and locked the vault when she went out for water? I just don't have any reason *not* to believe her. She's anal about everything, so it's hard to imagine she didn't follow procedures. She was adamant about that."

"But she could have forgotten, felt weak from the heat and wanted a glass of water fast, and just walked out. Then she could have lied about it because she is so fussy and didn't want anyone to know she had made a mistake."

"True. But that still doesn't explain how the vault got closed. Let's say she did leave it open, and I came in and went to look for the 'L' box. Believe me, there was absolutely no wind that could have closed the door."

"So she came back in, saw the vault was open, and slammed it shut. She was upset about her mistake and she didn't even see you in there."

"And I didn't see her because my back was turned to the door while I looked for the box. I guess that makes sense. But only if she was lying, and I just don't see that. She's weird, that's for sure, but somehow I can't see her lying about this."

"What's the alternative? Battles?"

"We can't overlook him. Here's what bothers me: After I told them I had found the letters in the 'L' box, he was awfully quick to say he remembered putting them there before. It was too convenient. Why didn't he think about LDS when we were looking under 'Y' and 'M' before?"

"There's another thing that bothers me about that."

"What?"

"You found the Brigham Young letters in the 'L' box. We looked through it when we were searching for the Lincoln letters."

"God, Rich, you're right. I hadn't thought about that. If the Young correspondence was there, we would have found it."

"Well, maybe not—we were so intent on finding the Lincoln letter and we didn't even know the Young letters were mising then, but I still think it's odd."

"Very odd," Julie said.

"Let's come back to Battles. How could he have been involved with the vault business?"

"Aside from rescuing me? I'm not sure."

"I'm not sure either, but that's one for me to think about. Meanwhile, anything else happen around here?"

"Let me back up and tell you about Mike Barlow," she said. "The police chief. And Worth and Martha Preston. Maybe we should go back out to the deck. You've got a long story ahead of you."

"Lucky I brought a bottle of cognac. Shall we?"

Rich tried to keep from yawning, but it was well after eleven, and two cognacs later, when Julie finished recounting the events of the last few days.

"Sorry, I'm boring you," she said when she saw him swallow his yawn.

"Far from it," he said, "but it is getting late."

"And you've had a long drive. It won't be like this all the time, Rich. Things will return to normal. But it's just been so strange. Let's get a good night's sleep and take a nice, long hike in the morning. I have to take that press release to the newspaper after I hear from the lawyer, but other than that I'm not going to do one bit of RHS business while you're here."

"Why do I think that's unlikely?" he asked. "Maybe because I know you too well," he answered, before she could.

The next morning, Julie received two telephone calls, neither of them hang-up calls. The first was from Henry LaBelle, giving his okay to the press release, and the second was from Dalton Scott, calling to invite Julie to brunch on Sunday.

"No RHS talk, I promise," he said.

Julie explained that Rich was in town. "Great," Dalton said. "I didn't get a chance to talk to him when you were here, but tomorrow it'll just be the four of us. How about noon?"

"Hope that's okay," Julie said to Rich. "You met Dalton last week at the Black Crow, but he was waiting tables and playing host. I know you'll really like him. And his girlfriend, Nickie Bennett; she's very nice, too—and gorgeous."

"That sounds like a great idea," Rich said.

Twenty-One

"Isn't it too hot for a hike?" Rich asked as they were having a leisurely breakfast.

"Probably," Julie said.

"How about kayaking instead? It'll be hot on the river, but we can dunk ourselves to cool down," Rich said. "I saw a rental place down by the river when I drove in last night."

"That sounds great! I can drop off the press release and then we'll get a kayak and spend the afternoon on the Androscoggin."

One disadvantage of kayaking, Julie thought as she and Rich headed out on the river, is that you can't talk much because in a double, you're both pinned in place. But maybe, she thought again, it's something of an advantage not to talk. Rich probably would appreciate a little peace and quiet after last night and her week's worth of talking, talking, talking. Moving along the water in silence had a certain appeal. Rich occasionally leaned back to say a word to her about the scenery, but otherwise he was as silent as Julie. He beached the kayak at a low spot where a side river joined the large one.

"What's up?" she asked.

"Damned blackflies," he said as he swatted at his neck. "It's time for a swim."

"For the heat or the flies?"

"Both. I really should have brought something to keep them off us."

"Part of the Maine scene," Julie said as she waved her hands to deter another of the creatures.

Rich began to do the same, and soon they were dancing around, waving their arms and swatting.

"Into the water!" Julie shouted.

Afterwards, they sat on the bank, watching the slow movement of the river. "It's really gorgeous, isn't it?" Julie said.

Rich nodded.

"All the little channels and waves flowing in together. Sort of like a puzzle," she said.

"Just like . . ." he began.

Julie finished for him—"Just like all that's happened the last week: the misplaced items, my phone calls, the vault. I can't help wondering if they're all connected in some way."

"What do you think? You're the puzzle-master."

"Thanks, Rich." She reached over and squeezed his arm—and swatted another blackfly. "I really appreciate your letting me talk this out. It helps."

"So go ahead. And keep swatting!"

"Well, maybe everything is connected, but maybe not. I mean, it's easy to think that because things happen around the same time, they're somehow related. But they don't have to be."

"Or they could be?"

"Right. Take the missing items: The Brigham Young letters have already turned up, so we know they're not related to the muskets or the painting and so on. What if the same is true of everything else—that even if they're missing, they went missing separately, on their own? So not a big theft but a series of misplacements and, maybe, thefts."

"Sure. It's possible that we're lumping together a bunch of separate things. Maybe everything will just show up. But what about the phone calls and your being locked in the vault? All separate incidents again?"

"Maybe yes, maybe no. I sort of think the phone calls and my vault experience are connected, and maybe they're also connected to one or more of the thefts, but that's just speculation. It's possible the calls were totally separate—some kid making random calls."

"But with caller ID you'll find out," Rich reminded her.

"And the calls have stopped. Remember Mike Barlow said that if someone knew I got caller ID, the calls might stop."

"And we know Jason Battles knows, right? So let's say he was doing it and then stopped because of ID."

"Okay, let's say that. Damn! These flies are horrible," she said as she waved off one and swatted another on her leg. "Anyway, what does it mean?"

"Well, it could mean we ought to think about whether he locked you in the vault. Let's assume Jason has the hots for you or something; he's a little strange, he makes calls, he finds out you're getting caller ID, and he stops the calls—and then he locks you in the vault."

"Why?"

"To scare the shit out of you. To get back at you for criticizing him about the painting and the letters, to show you that even if he has to stop making the calls, he can still get to you. Who knows? He's weird."

"Maybe—I just don't know," Julie said. She looked at her watch. We still have almost two hours to go before they meet us at the landing. Want to get going?"

At the next stop, they swam as soon as they beached the kayak.

Cooled by the dip, they sat on the bank. "How about a red herring?" Rich asked.

"Are you hungry again? I didn't pack any."

"Funny, funny. I was just thinking about our earlier conversation and whether the hang-up calls and locking you in the vault were both intended to divert attention from the thefts—or the thieves?"

"Possible," Julie said and stared at the river.

"Let's say they're not connected. And let's put aside the red herring issue for now."

"So the red herring is a red herring?"

"I still think it's possible, but you seem to be thinking about the vault. Go over that again."

Julie still found it hard to recount the experience, feeling the claustrophobia again as she described for the second time what had happened.

"So what do you think?" she asked when she was, thankfully, finished.

"It seems to me there are only two possibilities: either Battles locked you in, or Tabby did. And whoever did it either made a mistake or did it deliberately."

"I guess it's possible someone else came into the library, but you're right, it's probably either Jason or Tabby. I think we can eliminate Tabby. I just don't see any reason she'd deliberately lock me in, and I don't think she'd make a mistake about leaving the door open and then closing it to cover up."

"So you think Jason did it?"

"Why would he?"

"Say it's an accident—he doesn't mean to lock you in. Think about what he was like after he let you out—did he seem surprised? Did he act like he might have accidentally locked you in and then felt really relieved that he let you out?"

Julie pondered for a few seconds. "That would fit. It's possible."

"But also possible he had done it deliberately—and was also pleased you were safely out, and that he'd get the credit for that?"

"That's possible, too," Julie said. "Sorry, Rich, but I don't think I can sort this one out. And, I'm getting a little overwhelmed. Besides, I think it's time we headed for the put-out anyway. We don't want to miss our shuttle back to the kayak place. And I've had enough blackflies for one day!"

"And here I thought mosquitoes were the state bird of Maine!" Rich said.

Twenty-two

The Black Crow Inn was located halfway between the ski area and Ryland, on a knoll nestled below higher hills. Julie and Rich drove up the road from the main highway a few minutes before noon. On their first visit—Julie found it hard to believe it was just a week ago—it was too dark to appreciate the inn, but today they paused and looked it over.

"Should have realized he was an architect," Rich said, pointing to the two low, sleek wings that flanked the squat farmhouse. "The new and old really blend so nicely. Wonder why he decided to run an inn?"

"Maybe for the same reason I decided to run a historical society," Julie said. "To live in Maine."

"Could be. There he is," Rich said. Dalton Scott was standing near the front door of the main building.

"It's nice to see the inn in daylight," Julie said when they reached him. "You did such a great job with the new wings."

"Thanks," Dalton replied. "It was fun—and it gave me enough rooms to make an occasional profit. The old farmhouse just wasn't big enough. But it's the dead season now—no guests at all this weekend. Things will pick up when school lets out, but June is always slow. Anyway, I thought we'd eat outside, in the back where the sun hasn't gotten yet. Nickie's out there."

Dalton introduced Nickie Bennett to Rich and suggested Bloody Marys. "And no RHS talk," he said as he went back into the inn to get the drinks. They were making small talk when he returned with a pitcher and four glasses.

"So you knew each other before Maine?" Nickie said. "That explains a lot."

"Like what?" Dalton asked.

"Like why Julie took the job here."

"Partly," Julie said. "But I really wanted the job for its own sake. Something closer to Orono would have been more convenient, but this historical society has such potential."

"Violating the rule," Rich said. "Remember Dalton said 'no RHS talk.' "

"That's only for Julie's sake," Dalton said. "I don't want her to feel she has to talk shop. Especially with everything that's happened."

"Okay, Dalton," Nickie said. "That does it—the rule's suspended. You can't just say 'with everything that's happened' and then go back to normal conversation. I'm dying to hear about the thefts, Julie. Or is that all hush-hush?"

Julie laughed and agreed to give a quick report.

"I didn't know that!" Dalton said when Julie reached the point in her narrative about being locked in the vault on Friday morning. "You didn't mention it at the board meeting."

"I didn't think it was relevant then, and maybe it isn't. That's something Rich and I have been talking about."

"We're just trying to figure out if Julie's getting locked in the safe is connected to the phone calls, and if both of those are connected to the missing items," Rich said.

"What phone calls?" Nickie and Dalton asked simultaneously.

Julie explained.

"Wow, this gets more and more intriguing," Nickie said. "Who would have thought our little town could be so exciting?"

"Brunch is ready," Dalton said. "I'll go get it, and maybe you can stop talking about the Ryland Historical Society while I do."

"So you won't miss anything," Nickie said.

"Exactly."

"This is absolutely delicious, Dalton," Julie said as they ate quiche and salad. "You're a great cook as well as an architect and innkeeper."

"Thanks. I'm learning—you have to wear a lot of hats when you run a B&B. But can we get back to the vault?"

"I'd rather not be in the vault, but I don't mind talking about it, if it's not boring everyone."

And so for the next half-hour, as they finished their meals, they talked about the missing items and Julie's phone calls and vault experience. "Let me just get the flan," Dalton said when he saw they had finished. "The first strawberries of the season," he added. "Hope you like strawberry flan."

"So why would someone take all that?" Nickie asked, of no one in particular.

"How about money?" Dalton replied. "The muskets and the Lincoln letter are worth a lot, right? That newspaper story about professional thieves preying on historical societies seems pretty relevant."

"But how would they know where to look for the muskets?" Nickie asked.

"Good question," Julie said. "Professionals might guess the Society had something worthwhile. They could check that out, ask around. And eventually they'd talk to someone who knew Worth had moved the muskets—people at the Society aren't exactly unused to questions."

"But when did they do it?" Rich asked. "Do we know anything about that?"

"Sounds like a job for Mike Barlow," Nickie said.

"And what he would do," Dalton added, "is ask me and the other innkeepers around town about suspicious strangers who stayed here and asked about the historical society."

"Well? Were there any?" Nickie asked.

"Not that I can remember," Dalton said, "but then we're not sure of the time frame. The skiers are here in the winter, and leaf-peepers in the fall, and—as you can see—not many otherwise."

"So how about April?" Julie asked. "The painting seems to have disappeared around then."

"Let me just get the registration book." He returned quickly from the office and opened the book. "Let's see. I can sort of recall most of these folks in March and early April—late-season skiers. Then of course we were gone the last two weeks of April. I was going to close the inn, but Mrs. Potter said she'd handle things, and I think we had a few guests. Let's see: April twenty-third, two guests, John Albertson and Peter Shaw. Says they're from New York. Stayed just one night."

"Any address?" Rich asked.

"Not here—just New York. Doesn't say if it's the city or the state. Let me check how they paid. Help yourself to coffee or more flan. I'll just be a minute."

"Cash," Dalton said when he rejoined them. "Albertson and Shaw paid cash—not even a check. I'm going to call Mrs. Potter."

"Are you all sitting down?" Dalton asked when he returned. "Mrs. Potter remembered them, and they asked her about the Ryland Historical Society."

"Yes!" Julie said.

"Come on, now," Rich said. "Aren't we making too much of this? I mean, it's not a crime to stay at an inn and ask about the local historical society. And we don't know when the muskets were stolen."

"Still," Julie said, "you have to admit it's a pretty intriguing coincidence since the painting was last seen in April."

"I think I better call Mike Barlow," Dalton said. "I guess I should have enforced my no-shop-talk rule."

"Glad you didn't," Rich said.

When Dalton returned once again from the office, he reported that Mike Barlow was off for the day. The duty officer thought he had gone to Portland and offered to take the information and pass it on, but the innkeeper told him just to leave a message for the chief to call in the morning.

"Not much else we can do today," he said. "Anyone interested in a walk?"

"Not in this heat," Nickie said.

"We should really be getting home since Rich has to go back to Orono," Julie said. "This was a lovely brunch, Dalton, and it was really great to have a chance to talk to you, Nickie. I hope we can do it again—next time at my place."

"I'll let you know what Mike says," Dalton said as they stood beside Julie's car in the parking area. "Maybe we'll get those muskets back."

"Hope so," Julie said.

"Looks like you made some progress today," Rich said as they drove back to Julie's condo.

"Like I said, I hope so."

Despite the excitement of what they had discovered, Julie's mind wasn't on the stolen muskets.

"When do you have to leave?"

"About an hour ago, but if you're really nice I might stay a few more minutes."

Sunday evenings were the worst part of a commuting relationship, Julie thought as she straightened up the condo after

Rich left. The weekend's over, work looms, and another long week stands between you and him again. But next weekend she would go to Orono—she promised that this time she'd keep to the schedule, no matter what was happening at the Ryland Historical Society.

Rich called, as they had agreed, when he reached Orono. "You'll call, right?" he asked. "After Dalton talks to the cop. And in the meantime you won't worry about all this stuff."

"Right. Oh, Rich, it's tough doing this commuting."

"I know. We've got to talk about it."

"Next weekend in Orono."

"Right. Now you just relax. Keep the windows closed tonight. And call me when you go to bed. Or anytime."

She phoned him again at ten-thirty, reported that all was well, and that a storm was breaking out over the mountain.

"Scared?" he asked.

"No. Happy that this damned heat wave is going to break," she said and hoped it was true.

Twenty-three

Julie never had trouble sleeping in a storm. She found the rain lulling, and lightning and thunder didn't bother her at all. She snuggled into the covers, thinking of the cool air the storm would bring to replace the tropical conditions of the last few days. When she woke at six Monday morning, she rushed to the deck and found the promise fulfilled: the sun was bright but not scorching, and the crisp air almost autumnal. She felt reborn.

No need to walk early to beat the heat, she decided, and poured a cup of coffee.

She loved to sit on the deck and watch the colors of the mountain change in response to the moving sun. She would miss this view when she moved to Worth's house. She imagined the mountain peaks as pieces of a puzzle that she could take apart and reassemble.

But how were pieces of the other puzzle fitting together? Julie sighed. Well, it now seemed possible that professional thieves were responsible for some or all of the missing items. But how could they have known that the muskets were at Worth Harding's house? And how could they have gotten in and taken them without Worth knowing? Maybe Worth remembered the April visitors. And maybe the Society's visitors' log would show they had been there.

Julie jumped up from her chair, went into the kitchen, opened a vanilla yogurt and spooned it down as she gathered her clothes and prepared for a shower. In fifteen minutes she was on her way to Ryland.

From the office, she phoned Worth—no answer. She did not leave a message. Using the security code to open Ting House reminded her that the security company was coming today to change the code. Inside Ting, she went to the main desk and located the sign-in book.

Julie thumbed through the book until she found April, and ran down the dates to the 23rd. And there they were: "John Shaw, NYC," and below it "Peter Albertson," with a ditto mark below NYC. Was that right? She remembered the names differently. She was sure that yesterday Dalton had said John Albertson and Peter Shaw. She picked up the phone but realized she didn't know the number at the Black Crow Inn. She looked behind the counter, but couldn't find a phone book. Clutching the visitors' log, Julie closed the door behind her and jogged across the front lawns to her office in Swanson.

Relieved that Mrs. Detweiller wasn't yet at her desk, Julie looked at the pile of items on the table behind it and finally recovered the phone book.

Dalton Scott answered on the third ring. He consulted his records and confirmed her suspicion: the two guests signed in as John Albertson and Peter Shaw.

"That's it, Dalton!" she practically shouted. "The names had to be fake, and they forgot how they had registered at your place. Have you seen the chief yet?"

"He's coming by at noon. I think you should come, too."

"I'll be there," she said.

Jason Battles and Mrs. Detweiller arrived together. Julie wasn't sure how long they had been there. If they had heard her excited comments, neither let on.

"Heat wave's over," Mrs. Detweiller said matter-of-factly.

"Quite a storm, wasn't it?" Jason asked. "But worth it to get rid of that muggy heat. Hope you had a good weekend."

"Thanks; I did. Could I see you for a minute?"

Inside her office, Julie closed the door.

"Do you remember if you were working on the twenty-third of April?" she asked.

"I can check my calendar. Was that a weekend?"

"No. A Tuesday. I'm interested in two visitors that day," she said, handing the visitors' book to Jason. "These. Any chance you remember them?"

"It was a pretty slow day—only nine visitors all day. Or at least nine names in the book. Groups are recorded separately. Do you want me to check my calendar and see if we had any tours that day?"

"No. It's these two I'm interested in. Two men from New York. Does that ring any bells for you—like, did they ask to see anything in particular?"

"Whoa," Jason reminded her, "I'm still not positive I was here that day. Sometimes I take a weekday off in return for working weekends. Let me go check my calendar to be sure."

While Jason was out, Julie phoned Worth again. Still no answer. This time she left a message asking him to call her. Jason returned.

"Yeah, I was working that day. But it's hard to remember every visitor. Anything in particular about them that might help me remember?"

Julie was about to ask if the visitors had shown any interest in muskets or the Lincoln letter, but she suddenly decided that was not a good idea. "I don't know them, Jason, so I can't guess what they might have been interested in."

"Do they have something to do with the missing stuff?"

"It's complicated, but maybe you could think about it and let me know if you remember anything."

"I'll try," Jason said as he left her office.

"Mrs. Swanson for you," Mrs. Detweiller said from her desk as Julie was about to close her office door behind Jason.

"I'm just checking in, Julia, to see how you're doing," Mary Ellen Swanson said. Julie decided to ignore the woman's persistent misnaming of her. "What a shock that must have been!" she continued.

"Shock?"

"Yes, At the church vestry meeting last night, Dalton told me that you were locked in the vault last Friday. It must have been so frightening, dear."

"Fortunately, everything turned out okay."

"Saved by Jason Battles," Mary Ellen continued. "How fortunate he was there. Now, do you think it's connected to the rest of our—how shall I say this?—troubles?"

"Troubles?"

"Well, the thefts and all, dear."

"No, Mrs. Swanson . . ."

"Mary Ellen."

"Mary Ellen. No, I don't think they're connected."

Julie honestly wasn't sure herself, but she certainly didn't want to invite Mary Ellen into the speculations. She didn't know quite what to make of the woman, especially after the strange abstention from the vote about taking an inventory.

"Any progress, by the way?" Mary Ellen asked. "On the thefts?"

"Chief Barlow is looking into them, and he's put out an alert to other forces in case any of our items turn up at an antique store or something."

"Well, I'm sure things will turn up. There's usually a very innocent explanation, isn't there?"

Not always, Julie felt like saying but didn't.

"Tabby must have been a bit off her game," Mary Ellen continued without waiting for Julie's response. "She's such a stickler for rules; it's surprising she left the vault open with no one there."

"She said she closed it," Julie replied, "and I don't have any reason to doubt her. You're right about her being so careful."

"More than careful, frankly; she's a bit obsessive. Like her sister. They're two peas in a pod, those two. Have you gotten to know Martha yet?"

"I'm afraid it's been kind of hectic here. I really wanted to talk to Martha about the shop, but I just haven't had time. I hope to do it this week."

"Martha's an odd duck, my dear. Tread gently with her. She's had her share of problems, you know."

"No, I don't."

"Well, I certainly don't want to spread rumors, Julia, but I've heard that Martha might have had some sort of . . . well, mental problems before she came back to Ryland. But that's just a rumor, and the fact is, she has her own ideas about everything, especially if it concerns the historical society. Worth could tell you a thing or two about that."

"Worth?" Julie asked. She was wondering about Martha's "mental" problems, but really wanted to learn more about the woman's relationship with Worth.

"When it comes to how the Society is run, Martha and Worth never quite see eye to eye. Now, of course, I'm something of a newcomer myself to town, but one hears the stories."

"What stories, Mary Ellen?"

"Oh, they go back a long way, Worth and Martha. Grew up here, went through school together. Martha went away, and Worth stayed and started the Society. When Martha and Tabby moved back into the old homestead, they both got involved with the Society right away. Tabby seems to enjoy what she does, and heaven knows we're lucky to have her do it for free. But Martha never misses a chance to complain about Worth. She was mighty happy when he announced his retirement. I think she was hoping it meant he might be moving South, or at least moving out of Ryland. She mumbled something at a meeting once about making sure he returned things to their rightful owners before he left. But of course, he's not going anywhere. But I've got to run now, Julia. Let me know if anything else comes up. And stay out of the vault, dear!"

Julie faked a laugh and told Mary Ellen to take care. But as she hung up, she wondered if Martha's reference to returning things to their owners could have anything to do with the thefts. But surely, she would have brought that up already.

And what could Mary Ellen mean by Martha's "mental problems"? Julie still didn't know much about Worth and Martha's relationship.

But why does it matter? Julie wondered. What mattered was sorting out the New York visitors and getting to the bottom of the thefts. She called Worth again. Still no answer. It was such a gorgeous day, maybe he was out working in his garden. She decided to walk up to his house and check before driving to the Black Crow Inn to meet Chief Barlow and Dalton.

The garden behind his house was empty. There was no sign that he had been working in it. She walked around to the front and looked admiringly at the house. She just couldn't wait for it to be hers. She stepped onto the porch. The large front door was actually open a crack. She knocked anyway.

No response.

She knocked again.

Still no answer.

She pushed the door open a little further and called in.

Still no answer.

Unable to resist taking another peek at the house that would soon be her home, she opened the door all the way and stepped inside. She called out again.

Still no answer.

That's strange, she thought and turned toward the parlor before leaving.

She froze.

Worth Harding was home. He was lying on the floor beside the sofa. His body outlined by a pool of blood.

Twenty-four

Julie had never seen a corpse before, but she knew immediately that Worth Harding was dead.

Dry and faded, the blood outlined his body, especially his head, like a shadow. When they were growing up, Julie and her friends would lie on their backs in the snow and swing their arms and legs to make snow angels. That is what Worth looked like now. A snow angel—actually, a blood angel.

For some reason, she bent over him and yelled his name, even though she knew he was dead. She was going to bend down even more to feel for a pulse, but couldn't bring herself to touch his cold flesh. Instead, she slowly backed away from the dead body, away from all that blood, gagging, but willing herself not to vomit. And then she turned and sprinted down a hall that led to the kitchen.

She spotted the phone on the counter. She picked it up and dialed 9-1-1. She continued to gag and choke, even while explaining where she was and why she was calling. The dispatch put her through at once to Chief Barlow.

"I'm at Worth Harding's house and he's dead."

"Dead?" Mike asked. "Are you sure?"

"No, I didn't touch him. He's lying on the floor, in blood, and he didn't answer. I think he's dead. Hurry!"

"I'll be there in sixty seconds. Don't touch anything!"

Julie walked briskly from the kitchen and passed the parlor without looking in. She was on the porch when Mike's cruiser pulled up. The chief quickly got out and ran up to the porch.

"Stay here," he said brusquely and went inside. When he returned a few minutes later, he was speaking into his handheld radio.

"No siren," he said into the radio, and then added, "No hurry."

"Are you okay?" Mike asked Julie. "Why don't you come sit in the car for a minute?"

He took her arm and gently guided Julie to the cruiser. "Need some water or something?" he asked after he settled her into the backseat and stood at the open door.

"No, I'll be okay. Is he dead?"

"Afraid so. I hope you didn't spend too much time looking—not a pretty scene."

Julie began to sob.

"It's okay, Julie," Mike said. "Here, let me come in there and sit with you."

He walked around the vehicle and got in. He put his arms around her.

"Go ahead and cry—you'll feel better."

With or without the policeman's encouragement, Julie knew she was going to have a long, hard cry. It wasn't that she knew Worth well. But seeing him on the floor like that—and with the blood.

"All that blood!" she said through her tears. "What happened? Did he fall and hit his head?"

"Possible. We'll have to see. I called the rescue squad as a formality, but I'm sure they'll confirm that we should wait for the medical examiner. Sounds like they're on their way—despite my asking them to skip the siren."

The shrill sound of the pulsating siren grew louder, and Julie watched the ambulance with RYLAND TOWN RESCUE on its side come to a stop beside the police cruiser.

"Inside," Mike said to the driver. "And turn off that light, Jerry. I'll be right in.

"I need to go now, Julie," he said to her. "Are you okay here?

"I'll be all right, but you said it was possible Worth fell and hit his head. What did you mean? What happened?"

"We'll know after the ME gets here."

"But it wasn't . . . he didn't die a natural death?"

"I'm not a doc, or even an EMT."

"But you're thinking he was . . . that someone . . ."

"Let me just deal with the rescue guys first and secure the scene. Are you sure you're okay here?"

Julie said she was, and Mike quickly walked into the house. She sat quietly in the back of the cruiser until he and the two men from the rescue squad came out.

"It'll be at least an hour," Barlow stuck his head in the window to tell Julie. "I need to stay here till the medical examiner comes, but you don't. I can take your statement later."

"I'm really okay, Mike," she said. "I was on my way to Dalton Scott's to meet you and him and tell you what we think we found out about the robberies. We should let Dalton know we're not going to make it."

Barlow used his cell phone to call the Black Crow Inn and explain that something had come up that would keep him from making the noon meeting.

"I saw Julie in town and told her, too," he added. "No use explaining any more right now," he said to Julie after he ended the call to Dalton. "But like I said, you don't need to stay here."

"Why don't you take my statement now?" she asked. "While it's still fresh."

Barlow took notes as Julie told her story, beginning with her phone calls to Worth Harding that morning. "That's what Dalton and I were going to tell you," she said when she explained the reason she had wanted to talk to Worth so urgently. "We think two guys using fake names were in town in April. They came to the Society, and I wanted to ask Worth if he remembered them, and if they talked to him about the muskets."

"You can fill me in on that later," Mike said. "So you wanted to get in touch with Worth this morning, and after several calls you walked over here?"

"Right. I figured he'd be out in his garden, but he wasn't, so I tried the front door. It wasn't closed tight. I knocked several times, and eventually I guess I just knocked so hard the door swung open."

"You'd be surprised how many people in Ryland don't lock their doors."

"But with the things missing, like the muskets, you'd think Worth would have been keeping them locked now. "

"Maybe he did. Maybe he opened it to let someone in. But that's guessing. Go on. Tell me how you found him. Just take your time and try to remember all the details."

"At first I thought he had had a heart attack or something—that he fell and hit his head, because it was—I know this sounds crazy—but it was sort of flat on the side."

She shuddered.

"Anything else, Julie?"

She paused and closed her eyes. "I saw a pan or a skillet on the floor."

"Can you describe it?"

When she finished, he asked, "Did you see anything wrong in the house—anything that looked out of place, or moved around?"

"Like someone was going through the house? No. I was only there once before, and I really don't remember much. But I don't think I saw any tables turned over or cabinets open or anything like that."

"Anything else?"

"No, I don't think so. Oh my God. Do you think someone hit him with that pan?"

"I can't speculate, Julie," Barlow said, "and neither should you. I may have more questions for you later and if you think of anything else, be sure to track me down."

"What should I say back at the office?"

"Most folks will already know that Worth's dead. And soon they'll know all the details because Jerry, the EMT, eats lunch at the diner everyday. If folks know and start to ask you anything, just tell them you can't say anything. Tell them to talk to me."

When Julie walked into Swanson House, Mrs. Detweiller was standing beside her desk. With no pause or preface, she asked, "Who killed him?"

Twenty-five

"Jerry's my cousin," the secretary said in response to Julie's surprised look.

"Jerry?" Julie asked.

"He's the EMT—says he met you at Worth's. Naturally he'd call to tell me, after all the years I worked for Worth."

"Oh, right. Sorry, Mrs. Detweiller. I'm a bit stunned."

Julie noted that Mrs. Detweiller didn't share that condition. Her coldness was amazing.

"Finding the body, I'd guess so," the secretary replied.

"Chief Barlow told me not to talk about it yet."

"Everyone knows already."

Julie had no reason to doubt that. All she wanted to do now was to call Rich. She abruptly excused herself, leaving her secretary standing awkwardly in the middle of the room, and went into her office.

"Oh my God, Julie, that's horrible!" Rich said when she told him. "Are you okay?"

"I think so. I'll be okay."

"This is getting to be too much," Rich continued. "I'm really worried about you."

"About me? Why?"

"Jesus, Julie, what do you think? You get phone calls in the middle of the night. You get locked in the vault. Worth Harding is killed and you find the body. Something's going on there, and you're right in the middle of it."

"You're imagining that. I just happened to find Worth's body—that didn't have anything to do with me."

"I think I should come to Ryland," he said. "I'll call you after class. Meanwhile, promise me you'll stay public—don't be alone with anyone. Especially not Jason Battles."

"Jason? Okay. But don't worry, and please don't come here. I appreciate it, but I'll be fine."

"I'll talk to you right after class. Just do what I ask, please, Julie?"

Jason was standing by Mrs. Detweiller's desk when Julie walked out of her office. Like the secretary, he was somber but calm.

"It's terrible," he said. "Mrs. Detweiller was just filling me in. Are you okay? How did you find him?"

The question was making Julie impatient: Why was the concern directed her way, and not Worth's? "I'm fine. Chief Barlow asked me not to say anything for now, but I guess should inform the board."

"Mr. Townsend phoned while you were on the line," Mrs. Detweiller said without looking up. "He knows. He wants you to call him right back."

Julie went back to her office to place the call. Afterwards, she sat at her desk, looking out onto the Common. In the clear, bright sunshine, the grass was so deeply green that the scene seemed unreal. As unreal, Julie thought, as what had happened this morning. She shuddered. She wondered if she could ever live in Worth's house now, that image of his body burned into her mind. And what about Rich's concerns? She really did appreciate them, but she was also sure he was being unduly worried. She didn't feel unsafe, but when she looked at everything logically she could understand what Rich meant—there were a lot of strange things going on in Ryland, Maine. Among them was the oddly cool way in which both Jason and Mrs. Detweiller reacted to the news. Mrs. Detweiller's knock stopped Julie from pursuing that thought.

"Miss Preston was wondering if she could talk to you," Mrs. Detweiller said.

"I'll just go upstairs and see her."

"No, not that Miss Preston," the secretary corrected. "Martha Preston. She's over at the gift shop."

Martha was one of the last people Julie felt like talking with at the moment, but she was curious to see how Martha was taking the news. She walked over to the gift shop.

"Such a tragedy!" Martha said as soon as Julie walked through the door. "I'm sure it was a great shock to you, finding the body."

"It was, Martha, but Chief Barlow asked me not to discuss the details yet. I'm sure you understand."

"Yes, yes. Well, I just came by your office to see if there's anything I can do. I've known Worth all my life; he'd probably want me to help with his arrangements and so on."

"I wouldn't know about that," Julie responded, noting uncomfortably that Martha was getting teary-eyed. "It may seem like really bad timing, but maybe we should talk about the gift shop now?"

"Good for you to get your mind off things. Probably good for both of us," Martha added, forcing a smile. "Now, let me show you what we offer here—very nice items simply unavailable elsewhere. Very appropriate for our historical society."

Martha conducted her around the shop, gesturing at a shelf here and then abruptly turning to another there, speaking rapidly and then drifting into silence. Julie sensed that the woman was more upset than she had admitted, notwithstanding what Julie took to be Martha's odd relationship with the late Worth Harding.

The tour was rapidly turning out to be more about gift shops than Julie wanted to know, especially at a time like this: details about ordering, inventory, markups, deciding what would sell and what wouldn't. There was a manic quality to Martha's chatter.

"And we're very careful about the cash, let me assure you," Martha said. "No chance for hanky-panky here. I double-check the register and make sure we take all the cash to Mrs. Detweiller every day."

Julie realized this tour had no natural end. Martha could talk forever. Julie glanced at her watch.

"This has been very informative, Martha. I'd like to talk more, but I'm expecting a call right now and should get back to my office."

"Of course you have more important things to do now. But I'm glad you had a chance to see a little of the shop. We can continue this when you're more up to it. I'm sure it was very difficult for you, finding Worth like that."

Finding Worth like what? Julie asked herself as she made her way back to her office. That EMT—Jerry, she remembered—must have painted a vivid picture when he spread the word.

Twenty-six

"The security company is here," Mrs. Detweiller said when Julie stepped into the office. "Everything happens at once, doesn't it? She's waiting for you at Ting."

A young woman in a crisp khaki uniform with STATEWIDE SECURITY stenciled on the back was standing on a stepladder outside the main entrance to Ting House. Julie quickly introduced herself, and the woman climbed down the ladder to reciprocate.

"Nora Vachon, Statewide Security. I came to change your codes. I gather this isn't a great time, but I'm here and thought I'd better get started."

Even a visiting serviceperson seemed to know all about Worth. But before Julie could say anything out loud, Nora Vachon continued. "All those kids coming and going—I might be in the way, but that guy said it was okay to continue."

Looking up to see Jason leading a pack of schoolchildren around the side of Ting House, Julie realized that the security person wasn't referring to Worth's death.

"Sure, just go ahead," she said. "Do you need me?"

"I'll have some paperwork for you when I finish," Nora said. "But first, can you look at this code and verify that it's okay for me to make the change?" She extended a folded paper toward Julie. "Just open it and look to see it's okay, please."

Julie unfolded the page and saw the letters she had asked for: UDEL. "That's right."

"Okay, good; all I'll need from you besides your signature when I'm through here is a list of people who will have the new code. It's for the memory function. Whenever we change codes, we program the computer to remember all the wrong codes entered so we can keep track of how many times, and when, someone uses the old code. Sometimes when people change codes they forget to tell everyone who had the old code, and those people keep using the old ones, and that sets off the alarm. By collecting that information, we can remind you to get the new code to the right people."

"Got it," said Julie. "Just stop by my office when you're finished."

"Chief Barlow's here," Mrs. Detweiller said when Julie returned. "I'm just leaving. I told him to wait in your office, Dr. Williamson. And Mr. O'Brian called—the message is on the slip on your desk."

"Hope I'm not bothering you," Mike said as he rose to greet Julie. "How are you feeling?"

"I'm fine, really. I tried to avoid questions about Worth, but it seems everyone here knew already." As she spoke, she retrieved the pink WHILE YOU WERE OUT slip on her desk.

"Like I said, Jerry enjoys his lunch at the diner," Mike continued. "Don't worry. I'm used to it. I always say we don't need the newspaper as long as Jerry's head of Town Rescue."

Julie read the message: "Can't make Ryland today. Call me ASAP."

Good. She was glad Rich wouldn't be rushing to Ryland. She turned her attention back to Mike.

"Couple of matters I need to talk to you about, if this is a good time." She nodded. "The vault business, and the guys from New York you mentioned."

After they finished about the vault—her story, then questions and answers—Mike asked about the April visitors who had stayed at the Black Crow Inn and visited the historical society. Julie plunged into that tale, and when she was done she reminded him to talk to Dalton Scott.

"I'll do that," Mike said. "And you should go home and lock your doors and windows, and stay right there. Call me if you think of anything else, or if you need anything."

Although Julie didn't feel any precise concern for her own safety—nothing she could pin down or point to—the two warnings, from Rich and now Mike, did make her feel slightly nervous. "I'll be careful," she told the police chief.

Julie left a message at Rich's office and was in the process of leaving one on his home phone when Nora Vachon reappeared.

"Have you decided who will get the new code?" she asked.

"I'm afraid I haven't had time to think that through," Julie replied. "Who was on the old list?"

"Let's see. Worth Harding, Jason Battles, Howard Townsend, Martha Preston, Tabitha Preston, and Mrs. Detweiller," Nora read from the list.

"Mrs. Detweiller—no first name?" Julie asked.

"Nope. Just 'Mrs.' You want to keep all these on?"

"All except Worth Harding. They're all people who need to be able to let themselves in—but doesn't it seem like a long list to you?"

"Sort of, for a small place. But it's your call. If you want, we could just keep you on the list for now and you could add others later when you've had time to think about it."

"Well, it's too late to tell anyone else about the new code today, so as a practical matter I'm really the only one who knows. Okay, let's leave it that way, and I'll talk to people tomorrow and then send you the new list."

Julie signed the paperwork. "Maybe we could leave together," she said, picking up her briefcase and glancing around the office to make sure she had what she needed. "That way you can check me out on setting the code when we leave."

"That's just right," Nora said as she watched Julie key in the code for alarming the system. "I did the ones on Ting and Holder when I finished there, so everything's set. Ryland Historical Society is safe."

Twenty-seven

"I just couldn't escape," Rich said angrily. He called just a few minutes after Julie had gotten home. "Some guy was giving a lecture, and it's summer and there's hardly anyone around to fill the audience, and my department chair just happened to stroll by my office and mention the lecture to me, and I couldn't get out of it. But I could still come—I could be there in two hours."

"Don't be silly, Rich. Untenured faculty members should go to every lecture where they'll be seen."

"Tell me what's happened since we talked."

"So you don't really know any more about Worth Harding's murder?" Rich concluded after Julie finished her brief recital of the afternoon's events.

"Not really. But there's no reason for you to be worried about me. I'm locked in safely here."

"Like in the vault?"

"Not quite. And I'd just as soon forget that, thank you."

"But it happened, and the calls happened, and now this murder has happened. I really think I should drive over there."

"And what? Turn around and leave at six a.m. to be back in time for your class tomorrow? It just doesn't make sense. I'm a big girl. And I'm perfectly safe here."

Rich reluctantly agreed, although he told her he'd call her every hour through the evening. During the ten o'clock call, Julie told him she was going to bed but agreed she would phone him as soon as she woke. "It may be six," she warned him. "I seem to have adopted rural hours."

"If you don't call at six on the dot, I'll call you," Rich said.

So why is he calling now? Julie wondered as she swam up through her dreams and saw four-fifteen on the bedside clock. Groggy enough not to even think about the prospect of another hang-up call, she grabbed the phone.

"Statewide Security calling for Julie Williamson," the young male voice said.

"This is she."

"Can you give me the password, please?"

"Blue Hens."

"Okay," the man said. "I'm sorry to wake you, but your name was on the list to call right after the Ryland Police. Someone tried to use the old security code to enter one of your buildings—Swanson House. Because we just changed the code today, the computer kicked on the alarm. So it's probably not a break-in or anything, but the cop up there said he'd go by to check. Sorry about the hour."

"That's okay," Julie said. She was already up and reaching for the jeans she had dropped by the bed when she had crawled in. "Was it Chief Barlow you talked to?"

"Let me see. Yeah, Mike Barlow, he said. And he said to tell you he'd check it out and get in touch with you."

"Thanks. And I appreciate the call."

"Okay, Ms. Williamson. Hey, I see your code is UDEL, and your password is Blue Hens. Are you, like, from Delaware or something?"

"That's right. I didn't think many people around here would get that."

"Well, I went to UMaine, and we play Delaware in football, right? So I've seen the Delaware mascot—the Blue Hen, right? Don't worry. Your secret's safe with me."

Julie was in the bathroom when the phone rang again.

"Figured you'd be up, Julie," Mike Barlow said. "I'm outside your office, and everything's okay here. No break-in. But I guess the security service explained what happened—someone used the old code."

"What time was that? I forgot to ask."

"The alarm went off in their office at three-forty-five, and I got the call at home a couple of minutes later."

"I'm sorry, Mike. You don't need any extra problems right now."

"Happens all the time. We're short-staffed, and I was officially on call but thought I could get in a couple of winks. Anyway, you don't need to do anything. Have a good look around in the morning and let me know if you see anything weird."

"I'm already dressed. I'm headed out the door."

"Then, I'll stay here. See you in a bit. Be careful."

Now who would be trying to get into Swanson House at three-forty-five in the morning? Julie wondered.

"Glad no one's on patrol tonight," Mike said when Julie pulled up in front of Holder House and parked beside the police cruiser. "Probably would have stopped you for speeding."

"You said to be careful, but you didn't say anything about obeying the speed limit."

"True. Anyway, want to have a look inside? I'll go with you. I walked around and checked all the windows from the outside."

"Can you just shine your light on this for me?" she asked, pointing to the security pad by the door.

Barlow held his flashlight above his head to focus it on the keypad. Julie punched in the code.

"What this?" Barlow said. The light illuminated more than the security pad. Just beside the step was something plastic that gleamed in the circle of the policeman's flashlight. He stooped to retrieve it. "One of those zipper bags with something in it."

"A. Lincoln!" Julie exclaimed. The famous signature was visible at the bottom of the page inside the plastic. "It's the letter—Lincoln's letter to Hannibal Hamlin!"

"Could be," Barlow said. "Certainly looks like an old letter. Let me get something to pick it up with."

He returned from the cruiser with a pair of kitchen tongs. "Pretty useful," he explained to Julie as he picked up the plastic bag with the tongs. "Let's go inside and have a better look."

"I never saw it, but I'm sure it's the missing letter," Julie said after Barlow placed it on her desk and turned it once with the tongs. "That signature is so familiar."

"It sure does look like 'A. Lincoln.' Wonder why he didn't write out his first name?"

"I have no idea," Julie said. "But let's open this so I can see if it's addressed to Hamlin."

"Not right now. I want to dust this for prints first. I better take it right to the office. Do you want to look around here?"

"If all the windows are okay, there's probably no need to. I think I'm beginning to figure out what happened here, Mike."

"Good. You can explain it to me. I'm all ears, but I'm also all stomach—would you like to have breakfast and tell me what's going on? The Greek opens at five."

"The Greek?"

"The diner out on the highway. Opens for breakfast at five, and I'm starved. Let's lock up here, and I'll take this plastic bag to the office and meet you there. You know where it is?"

Julie had driven by the diner dozens of times but hadn't thought to stop. It was not exactly an inviting place—a one-story concrete block structure that could have been an auto-body shop or a dry cleaner. Not that she had seen either of these businesses in Ryland. But right now the thought of a cup of coffee and a high-cholesterol diner breakfast sounded divine. "See you there," she said and drove off.

That's why she hadn't made the connection, Julie told herself as she parked in front of the diner and looked up at the sign that said BERT'S FAMILY RESTAURANT. By the time Barlow joined her, Julie was already sipping her coffee from a large mug that said THE FOOD PLACE.

"So how come it's called The Greek?" Julie asked the chief when his coffee, also in a FOOD PLACE mug, arrived almost as soon as he sat down.

"Thanks, Lou," the policeman said to the man who had brought the steaming mug. "I guess it's not," he said to Julie. "I still call it that because when I was a kid, the family who ran it were Greek. So we all called this place The Greek."

"How about 'The Food Place'?"

"Well, that came later, I think. And then Lou bought it."

"What about Bert?"

"How do you know about him? I nearly forgot."

"That's what the sign outside says," Julie responded.

"Does it? Anyway, Lou's been running it for three or four years."

"Five," the man standing by their booth corrected Mike. "Time goes fast when you're having fun. Usual, Mike?"

"Sure, and, Lou, let me introduce Julie Williamson, the new director of Ryland Historical Society."

Lou wiped his hand on his apron and extended it. "Pleased to meet you," he said. "What can I get you?"

Julie ordered—scrambled eggs, crisp bacon, and an English muffin.

"Grilled or toasted?" Lou asked.

Julie stared at him blankly.

"The English—you want it grilled or toasted?"

"Toasted, I guess. I didn't know you could do it any other way."

"Most people like grilled—it gets some of the fat from the grill that way," Lou said. "But toasted is fine by me. Potatoes with that?"

"Sure."

"Home fries or grilled?"

"Grilled. And can you grill the English muffin, too? Guess I should be consistent."

After Lou left, Barlow told Julie he had been late because he decided to do a quick dust of the plastic bag containing the letter. "Not definitive," he said, "but it looks clean. Whoever left it must have been wearing gloves, which makes sense. But I'll send it to Augusta for a full test anyway."

"With the letter?" Julie asked.

"Sure, I'll have to send the whole thing to them, but after I did the dust I opened the envelope with the tongs and pulled out the letter—three pages. And it's to Hannibal Hamlin."

"That's great! Having that back really makes me happy. I had this awful sense that if we lost that letter, we lost a piece of history. You didn't happen to notice what it was about, did you?"

"Didn't really look closely—probably wouldn't have understood it anyway. I figured you knew something about the contents."

"Not at all. As far as I can tell, only Worth had actually read it, and he never said. And, of course, now . . . Well, I guess when it comes back from the lab I'll get a chance to read it."

"That could take a while. Anyway, looks like one more missing item isn't. Now you said you were thinking about what happened. Since my stomach's about to be taken care of, my ears are ready."

Lou laid the plates before them, and Barlow tucked into his omelet. "But go ahead and start yours," he said.

Between bites, Julie told Barlow what she had puzzled over as she drove to the diner. "It's pretty simple," she began. "First, someone who knew the old security code tried to use it to get into Swanson House."

"Who knew the code?"

"Worth."

"We can eliminate him—so to speak."

"Right. Then me."

"Let's eliminate you, too—in a different way, of course."

"Thanks. Okay, that leaves Jason Battles, Martha Preston, Tabitha Preston, Howard Townsend, and Mrs. Detweiller. I know for sure because the woman from Statewide Security had the list this afternoon—or yesterday, I guess it was."

"Battles was there as much or more than Worth," Barlow said, "so that makes sense. And your secretary and Howard would be on the list. Why the Preston sisters?"

"Well, they're practically employees, although they're both volunteers—Tabby in the library, and Martha runs the gift shop."

"Okay, so unless one of them gave the code to someone else, it must have been one of those five who keyed in the old one tonight."

"And left the letter," Julie added.

"Not sure I follow that," Barlow said as he wiped his plate clean with the last piece of toast.

"Why else would the letter be there?" Julie asked.

"I can think of lots of ways—someone put it there, at some point. But it doesn't follow automatically that it was the same person who used the old security code, or even that it was tonight. That letter could have been there for days. We found it because I was using the flashlight so you could see the security keypad. It was down there along the steps, not easy to see unless you're looking for it."

"I still think it was left there tonight. I think someone was going to return it, someone who had the code and planned to enter in the middle of the night and put the letter back. But when the code didn't work, the person panicked and left the letter to get rid of it, to get out of there before anyone came in response to the alarm and found him, or her, with the letter."

"Theft in reverse?" Barlow asked.

"I guess you could call it that."

"But why?"

Twenty-eight

"I've got to make a phone call," Julie said instead of answering Barlow's question. "Is there a pay phone here? My cell phone doesn't seem to work around Ryland."

"You can use mine. It works only in Ryland, as a matter of fact. Once I get out of town, no reception." He held his cell phone out to her. "Seems kind of early to make a call, though."

"My boyfriend is supposed to phone me at six at home. I better call him now because if he tries me at the condo, he'll be worried when I don't answer."

"It might work better outside, if you don't mind taking it out to the parking lot. Like I said, reception's not great."

The call took longer than Julie had expected. Rich listened patiently. When she was done, he said, "That's it, Julie. I'm coming to Ryland today."

Mike was finishing his second cup of coffee when Julie returned.

"It was a little more complicated than I realized, explaining things to Rich," she said. "Sorry you had to wait."

"I've just been thinking about what you said," Barlow answered. "Nothing like a good breakfast and lots of coffee to stimulate the brain."

"What have you been thinking?"

"That you're probably right about how the letter got there. It seems too much of a coincidence for it to just end up by the steps that way. But I still have that question I asked before—why would someone want to return it in the first place?"

"Well, maybe the person found the letter and wanted to get it back without our knowing who had taken it. Or the person took it and felt guilty—or scared, or just nervous."

"Had second thoughts about being a thief?" Barlow asked skeptically.

"Possibly."

"Yeah, I'll grant that it's possible, but in my experience people don't often return what they stole."

"Maybe we shouldn't keep thinking the Lincoln letter was stolen in the first place. Maybe it was like the Brigham Young letters—taken to be used and then returned."

"I thought Battles had just misfiled them."

"That's what he says, but actually I've had some thoughts about that, too."

"And if I had a third cup of coffee I'd be ready to listen to them. Lou? Another round over here, please."

When Julie looked up as Lou refilled their cups, she realized that while she and Mike had been talking, the diner had come alive. Only one person had been there when she had arrived—a man sitting by himself at a table near the back. Now every booth and all but one table were occupied. "Maybe we shouldn't be talking here," she said.

"Folks are too busy eating and chatting to hear us," Mike said, "but you can be sure that everyone in town will know you had breakfast with me this morning."

"So should I tell you about the vault?"

"Does this have to do with the letters?"

"Yes, the Brigham Young letters. Jason was using them for an article he's writing, and he said he'd returned the file, although we couldn't find it last week. But it *was* there Friday.

So what if Jason came to the library to return the letters when I was there and then . . ."

"Locked you in? Why?"

"I don't know. Maybe it was an accident. Maybe he didn't know I was in the vault. But I just didn't believe him when he said he had filed the Young correspondence under 'L' and had forgotten it. Besides, the letters weren't in the 'L' box when Rich and I were looking for the Lincoln letter. Which has to mean that someone, maybe Jason, put the Young letters back later."

"So you're saying that Battles has a habit of returning things when you find out they're missing?"

"I hadn't put it all together that way before, but it is possible, isn't it? Maybe he had come in when Tabby wasn't there, used his key to open the vault and replaced the letters. But before he could close the vault, he heard me coming and hid. And then he closed the vault, not realizing I was inside. That must be it!"

"Now don't get so excited," Mike cautioned. "I see your point. But we don't know for sure. And even if Battles replaced those letters, it doesn't mean he was trying to put the Lincoln letter back. He could do that anytime—just like with the Young letters."

The excitement Julie had felt as she spun out her theory about Jason was gone. She felt deflated. "You're right. I don't know."

"Well, one thing I know is that if I don't get back to the station the taxpayers of Ryland will be looking for a new police chief. Let me get this," he said, and picked up the bill that Lou had left when he had brought the last round of coffee.

"I can do that," Julie said.

"Can't let citizens buy me breakfast," Mike said, "and yours is a business expense. You can leave the tip if you want."

Mike went to the cash register to pay, chatting briefly along the way with several customers. Julie was waiting outside, and when Mike emerged she asked what he was going to do next.

"A talk with Jason Battles seems in order," he said. "When does he get in?"

"Early," Julie said, looking at her watch. "Any time now."

They drove separately. Julie followed Mike's suggestion that she go directly to her office so he could find Jason without revealing that they had been talking. But when Julie walked toward Swanson House after parking her car, she was surprised to see Jason sitting on the step.

"Locked out," he said. "I saw the woman from Statewide yesterday afternoon and figured she was changing the codes. I didn't want to set off an alarm or anything."

"I'm sorry, Jason," Julie said. "I didn't have a chance to give anyone the new code yesterday."

Jason stood back, seemingly uninterested, as Julie punched in the new code and then unlocked the door to let them in. "I'll just write down the new code for you," she said as they entered the office together. "Let me grab a pen."

There was a soft knock on the door frame.

"Excuse me," Mike said. "I hope I'm not interrupting a meeting. I was just looking for Jason Battles."

"No meeting, Chief," Julie said.

"Then I wonder if we could talk, Mr. Battles?" Mike continued.

"Sure," Jason said. "We can go to my office."

Julie called Rich at work.

"He was covering himself," Rich said after Julie told him about Jason waiting outside the office because didn't know the new code. "When it didn't work last night, he left the letter and ran because he figured out there was a new code and the old one would alert the security company."

"He was here when the woman from the company was doing the work yesterday," Julie countered, "so it makes sense that he knew there was a new code—without having tried it this morning."

"Could be," Rich said. "But making a big thing out of waiting for you—to me that really sounds suspicious."

"Well, Mike Barlow is interviewing him now."

"About?"

"He didn't tell me."

"Okay. Just promise me you'll stay away from Battles. I'll be there by five—will you still be at your office?"

"I'll stay until you get here."

Twenty-nine

To occupy herself while she waited for Mike Barlow to finish with Jason, Julie distributed the new security code to the three others at the Society who knew the old one. Howard Townsend, she thought, could wait.

Mrs. Detweiller responded to the information as she had to everything Julie had done since becoming director. "There was nothing wrong with the old one," the secretary said, "and I'm not sure I can remember anything this complicated. Well, I seldom need the code anyway, so I'll just leave this in my desk."

She opened a drawer and tossed in the paper on which Julie had written the code. "Don't worry, I lock my desk when I leave."

Julie debated whether to point out that having the code in the desk drawer wasn't going to be of much use to Mrs. Detweiller in the event she needed it to get into Swanson House. Instead, she said, as she left the office, "I'm going over to the gift shop to give the code to Martha Preston. So if Chief Barlow is looking for me, would you tell him where I am?"

Martha was behind the counter when Julie came into the shop. "We have a busload of seniors this afternoon," she said. "I like to move the toys right up front for them."

When Julie expressed her surprise, Martha explained in a tone that mixed delight with contempt. "Toys," Martha repeated.

"I still don't follow, Martha. I assumed the school groups would be the target for the toys."

"Well they are, of course—or the toys are the target for the children; we do have to be so careful about young people these days, forgetting to pay and that sort of thing. But the seniors are the biggest buyers of our toys. They buy little things for their grandchildren. So I put these right up where they can see them. It's little things like this, you see, that make the difference between success and failure in retail."

"I have a lot to learn about the gift shop."

"Yes, you do; but what can I do for you this morning?"

Julie handed her a paper with the new code and was about to explain it when Martha said, "A new code, of course."

"Of course what?" Julie asked.

"Oh," Martha said, "that woman who was here yesterday."

Julie noticed that Martha seemed flustered, but she regained her composure as she continued. "I saw her up on a ladder by Ting House when I was leaving. Couldn't figure out what she was doing. All projects are approved by the board of trustees, and I didn't remember any discussion, but I see now—you were having the security code changed."

"That's right. Chief Barlow suggested it, because of the missing items, and the company said they'd recommended it to Worth, but he hadn't gotten around to it."

"No, he wouldn't," Martha said. "Well, I'll just put this in my purse. Thank you. And you don't need to worry; just because Tabby and I are sisters, it doesn't mean I tell her everything. I'll keep the code to myself."

"As a matter of fact, I'm on my way to see Tabby right now to give her the code."

"I don't know why she'd ever need it!" Martha sniffed. "But apparently it's not a board matter. It's your decision."

You're damned right it is, Julie said to herself after leaving the gift shop. I am the director, and deciding who gets the code is my business. She may be a trustee and a volunteer, and call her an "odd duck" or whatever, but Martha was someone Julie was finding pretty intolerable.

Tabby Preston was sitting at her small desk in the middle of the library, looking at a stack of papers. She practically jumped out of her chair when Julie spoke her name.

"Oh, sorry—I didn't hear you come in."

"I didn't mean to startle you, Tabby. You looked busy. How's everything going?"

"I'm just trying to sort out some correspondence here—letters from the doctor who had the house over there." She pointed out the window to the Common. "He was in practice here when I was a child, though he was ancient even then. Well, anyway, his daughter left us all his papers, and Worth wanted me to organize them. They're really quite interesting."

Julie explained about the new security code and handed a paper to Tabby. "It's really pretty easy," she said, "so perhaps you could just memorize it and then throw this away, or put it somewhere safe."

"I don't really need it," Tabby said, and without looking at the paper returned it to Julie. "I'd rather not have it, frankly. I never come into Swanson House by myself. Never have and don't expect to," she added firmly. She looked down at the papers on her desk and ran her hands across them nervously, straightening them into a neat pile.

"Are you sure you don't want the new code?"

"Absolutely not. But perhaps . . ."

"Yes?"

"Well, there is something I would like to discuss with you, if you have time; but maybe this isn't the right time—or place. Perhaps we could meet in your office, unless you're busy right now . . ."

Tabby's sudden desire to have a private discussion struck Julie as odd, but intriguing. "This is a perfect time, Tabby."

"Are you sure?"

"Why don't we go down to the office right now?"

Tabby rose from her chair. "I'll just put these together and get them into the vault."

Julie elected to wait by the main door while Tabby carried the papers into the vault. She pulled the door shut and was inserting the key to lock it when Chief Barlow opened the door from the stairs, nearly hitting Julie.

"Oh, sorry," he said. "Your secretary said you were up here. Can we talk for a minute?"

Julie looked at Tabby. "It's quite all right," Tabby said. "I can just go back to work on these, and you can let me know if you're free later. I really don't want to bother you."

"It's no bother. I'll come up when we finish."

"It's a little tricky discussing a case with someone," Mike began as soon as Julie had shut her office door and taken a seat beside him at her worktable, "but you're up to your neck in this, so I have to tell you a couple of things."

"Don't tell me anything you shouldn't."

"The main thing is that I didn't get any really good answers from Battles. I want to have him interviewed by a detective from the State Police, if I can get one up here tomorrow. I told him that, but he said he wanted to talk to a lawyer."

"Really?" Julie was surprised. "Does he think you suspect him of—well, what *do* you suspect him of?"

"I didn't say I suspected him of anything."

"But you do."

"Look, I'm only telling you this because first, you're the director of the historical society and his boss, and if he had anything to do with the missing items you should know. And second, I'm still concerned about your safety, after the phone calls and your being locked in the vault."

"You think he did those things?"

"He denied both, but there was just something in the way he answered that bothered the hell out of me. Can't say what it was, but I don't trust him. And he doesn't have an alibi for either time."

"Either?"

"Sunday night and last night."

"Why Sunday night?" Julie asked, and then it quickly dawned on her. "Oh my God—you think he killed Worth?"

"I didn't say that."

"I thought you were just focusing on last night, when the letter was left outside. I didn't get a chance to tell you earlier, but Jason said this morning that he was waiting for me to open the building because he didn't want to use the old code."

"Now that's interesting. Tell me again what he said." Mike took out his legal pad and wrote as Julie tried to recall exactly what Jason had said.

"He said he had seen the woman from Statewide and just assumed the codes were changed, but I think that's suspicious."

"You think he found out about the new code at three-forty-five this morning?"

"I think it's possible. That would explain why he didn't try to get in this morning by using the old code."

"It would. I wish I had known this before I talked to him."

"That's my fault, Mike. I didn't want to say anything in front of him."

"No problem."

"You said Jason didn't have an alibi for this morning or for Sunday," Julie reminded Mike.

"Right. He's got two stories, but no one to verify either one. Sunday he says he was in Portland, doing the bar scene, and drove home late. But he can't come up with anyone who can confirm that. So far. Maybe by tomorrow he will. And last night he was home in bed. Anyway, I may have stepped over the line on this, but I told Battles he should go home and stay there until I contact him about meeting with the State Police. I don't want him around the historical society—or you—today."

Julie was startled. "Is there something else I should know?"

"Just trust me, will you? By the way, is Battles left-handed?"

"Left-handed? I haven't noticed. Is that important?"

"Just something I'm thinking about. Noticed he wears his watch on his right hand."

"What's the deal about being left-handed?"

"Look, I should keep my mouth shut, but I'm concerned about your safety and want you to take this seriously."

Mike paused to look at Julie, fixing her eyes. "Here's the thing: I'm pretty sure Worth Harding was killed by someone who's left-handed. I still have to get confirmation from the ME."

"Because he was hit on the right side of his head! I get it. With the skillet? And you think Jason did it?"

"There weren't any prints on the skillet, so the murderer either wore gloves, which implies premeditation, or did an excellent job of wiping them off," the chief said. "I don't think I have to tell you again how important it is to keep this to yourself, and stay away from Battles."

"Don't worry about me," Julie said with a smile. "My boyfriend is coming over from Orono today—he's meeting me here at five."

"Good." Mike began to leave but hesitated. "One more thing I guess I better tell you." Julie nodded at him. "It's sort of tricky, but Battles made a big point of saying that you were going to get Worth's house."

"I'm not getting the house. The historical society is."

"But you'll be living in it."

"Right. Although I'm not sure if I can live there now knowing Worth was killed there. All that blood . . ." Julie gave a little shiver. "But I don't understand what Jason meant."

"He was hinting that you have something to gain from Worth's death."

"That's ridiculous."

"I think crazy is what I said," Mike corrected her with a smile that made her laugh.

Thirty

Julie stayed at the worktable after Mike excused himself. Was she really in danger from Jason? Could the assistant director have actually murdered his former boss? And why did Jason raise the issue of Worth's house? Because he really thought she might have killed him? Or, as Mike suggested, to deflect suspicion from himself?

Suddenly, Mrs. Detweiller was standing before her.

"It's not at all like Jason," she said, "but then, nothing's been the same around here since . . ."

Julie stopped her secretary before she concluded with what Julie was sure would be a criticism of her directorship. "What's not at all like Jason, Mrs. Detweiller?"

"Leaving just like that, in the middle of the day, when he has a tour to give. He's a very responsible young man. This is just not the kind of thing he would do. There must be something terribly wrong."

"It's okay. I know about it," Julie said.

"I suppose it has to do with Chief Barlow."

Julie smiled and asked, "What time is the tour?"

"It's at one-thirty, a senior-citizen bus tour from New Jersey or Ohio or some other place in the Midwest. Someone will have to greet them and do the introduction. Jason is so good at that."

"I'm sure he is, but I'll take care of it."

"*You*, Dr. Williamson?" Mrs. Detweiller said derisively, as if Julie considered herself too important for such tasks.

"That's right. I'd be happy to welcome a busload of senior citizens. And you don't need to worry anymore about that, Mrs. Detweiller. Everything's fine."

"I can't believe it," Mrs. Detweiller said.

It was ten minutes past one when Julie entered Holder House and spoke cheerily to Martha, who stood guard at the door to the gift shop.

"Due any minute," Martha said, looking like a cat about to witness the beginning of a mouse parade. "The tour starts at one-thirty, but the bus has to get here fifteen or twenty minutes before that so people have time to get off and get assembled. Where's Jason?"

Julie explained that Jason had gone home for the day and she was substituting for him.

"*You*?" Martha Preston screeched in what Julie considered a perfect imitation of Mrs. Detweiller's tone and disbelief.

"Yes, me," she responded, hoping the simplicity of the response would add to the authority she tried to infuse in it.

"I hope nothing's wrong with Jason. He's a fine young man, even though Worth doesn't think so. I always stick up for Jason when Worth criticizes him," she said. "Worth won't be picking on Jason anymore, will he?" she added in a tone Julie found oddly out of sync with the reality of Worth's recent, and violent, death. "And, there's your bus. Good luck."

Julie turned to look at the bus that had stopped in the parking area and was slowly disgorging a line of women in polyester pantsuits and men in golf shirts. They stepped down one by one, and then formed into small groups, pointing at the buildings and talking among themselves. Julie felt that a switch inside her had been flipped. She put Jason Battles and Martha Preston out of her mind and suddenly became the director of the Ryland Historical Society. She walked confidently toward the first group, her arm extended to shake hands with her guests.

Julie herded the seniors into the visitors' center in Holder House, a large room with exhibits and wall panels depicting the history of Ryland. After formally introducing herself and welcoming the tour group—which, she had learned during the conversations outside, was from Scranton, Pennsylvania; so much for Mrs. Detweiller's sense of geography—Julie launched into a brief history of the town, pointing to prints and artifacts to illustrate the points she was making about Ryland's founding after the Revolution, its early agricultural traditions, and the later shift toward lumbering and the wood-products industry. She may have been rusty on the KKK, but, she thought proudly to herself, she obviously had retained quite a bit of local history from the heavy reading she had done in the months between her appointment and her arrival in town.

"What about the muskets?" a heavy man standing toward the back of the group asked.

"The muskets?" Julie repeated.

"Yeah, the brochure said you had Revolutionary War muskets—used by Benedict Arnold's expedition against Quebec. I'd sure like to see those. I'm a collector."

"Well, we do have two very fine muskets," Julie said. "Unfortunately, they're being restored at the moment, so they're not going to be available for viewing today. I'm sorry about that, sir, but perhaps I can arrange to have some photos of them sent to you."

"That's okay," he said glumly. "I've got lots of pictures."

Apologizing to the man again, Julie resumed her talk. At the end, she said, "Thank you for your attention. I'd be happy to answer any other questions you may have, and in a few minutes one of our guides will take you into Ting House for a very special tour. It's a fine period home, extremely well maintained and furnished in authentic pieces. I'm sure you'll enjoy it."

After Julie answered a few questions, she took the opportunity to speak to the musket man. She asked him where he'd read about the guns.

"Right here," he said and pulled a Xeroxed copy of a two-fold brochure from his windbreaker. Sure enough, the old brochure talked about "two very fine examples of Revolutionary War musketry" as being among "the gems of the Ryland Historical Society's extensive and historically significant collections."

She asked the man if she could borrow the brochure to copy it. When she returned, one of the volunteer guides, Ben Marston, was getting the group ready for the house tour. Julie decided to tag along. "Glad to have you," Marston said when she asked if it was okay with him. "I'm sorry I haven't been by to say hello yet. My wife and I just got back from vacation two days ago. And poor Worth, what a shock, eh?"

Marston had a nice line of patter, friendly and welcoming but very accurate on historical issues and artifacts—at least as far as she knew, she reminded herself. On the second floor, one of the visitors pointed to a door near the back stairs and asked where it went. "It goes to a small room, and we don't really know for sure what it was used for," Marston said. "Probably a little getaway room for the mistress of the house, maybe a kind of office where she kept bills and things. We usually don't show it on the tour because it's too small for everyone to fit in there, but you're a special group, so I'll open it up for you."

Dutifully, each and every one of the seniors, happy to have this special look, took turns squeezing into the room and then backed out to allow the next in. "What a lovely painting," a woman said to Ben Marston, who had stationed himself outside the door. "Do you know who the artist is?"

He stepped inside to look at the painting. "Oh, that one," he said. "It's a very nice watercolor of Ryland done in the 1840s, I think. It used to hang downstairs."

Thirty-one

How and why the formerly missing painting ended up in the small room on the second floor of Ting House should interest her, Julie knew. But what interested Julie most at the moment was verifying the painting against the inventory card. She excused herself from Ben Marston's tour and returned to her office. She checked the entry. There was no question that the painting was one and the same.

Last week when they had discovered the painting was gone, Worth told Jason to look through the house for it and talk to the volunteers. Why hadn't Jason checked the little room? Maybe he had, Julie thought. She phoned the police chief to fill him in.

"That's a coincidence," Barlow said. "I was just going to call you with some good news—the muskets have been found, all four of them."

"You're kidding!"

"Nope. An antique store in Albany, New York—they got the bulletin from their local police and recognized the guns. Bought them from two guys in May. And now that you've located the painting, that pretty much takes care of the missing items."

"Except for the Klan outfit," Julie reminded him.

"The way things are going, maybe it'll turn up, too."

"When will we get the muskets back?"

"I need to coordinate that with New York, but they're safe for now, and frankly, that's not at the top of my list."

"Jason Battles is?" Julie asked.

"Worth Harding's murder is."

"Of course. I'll let you get to it," Julie said.

After calling Howard with the good news about the muskets, Julie checked her watch. Rich would be arriving in about two hours. She was grateful for the time, because a large stack of paperwork had piled up. Mrs. Detweiller had been reproachfully adding to it each day. It felt good to tackle it, and the time passed quickly. Julie was startled when Mrs. Detweiller knocked and entered.

"I'll be leaving now since it's four-thirty, Dr. Williamson. I didn't want to disturb you while you were working, but Tabitha Preston came by several times to see you. She said she'll stay on in the library if you get a chance to come up."

Julie had completely forgotten about poor Tabby. She stuck a Post-it on the front door, directing Rich to come up to the second floor when he arrived. In the library, she found Tabby just as she had last seen her, hunched over her desk and working with the doctor's correspondence. "I'm so sorry, Tabby. How are those letters coming?"

"These?" the woman said and glanced down at the pile in front of her as if she had never seen them before. Clearly she was distracted. "Oh," she added, "they'll take time. But I'd like to talk to you about the other letter."

Julie watched silently as Tabby Preston rose from her desk and began walking slowly around the room, rubbing her hands together and occasionally stopping and then abruptly resuming her aimless strolling. Julie couldn't shake the blue-heron image.

"What letter?" Julie prodded.

"The one from President Lincoln," she said almost inaudibly.

For an instant Julie forgot whether she had told anyone that the Lincoln letter had been recovered earlier that morning. Except for Rich and Mike Barlow, she was sure no one else knew. "What about it?" she asked.

"I shouldn't be telling you this. With Worth dead. Maybe I should talk to the police first. I just don't know . . ."

"If you know something, you can tell me, and of course we'll tell the chief. Do you know where the letter is, Tabby?"

"Well, not exactly." The woman got up and began pacing again, directionless, wringing her hands together. Julie waited. "Not exactly," she repeated as she moved toward the window and stared out. "Just what Worth told me."

"Worth told you where the letter is?"

"Yes."

"When?"

"On Sunday. At his house."

"You were at Worth's house on Sunday?" Julie asked gently.

"Yes. I've been very upset about what's been happening here—all those items missing. It's just not the way we do things. I was afraid."

"What were you afraid of?"

"That someone would think I wasn't doing my job. So I wanted to talk to Worth about what had been going on. You know he had the muskets, which I thought was wrong, but he felt they would be safe at his house. So I wondered if he had put other things there."

The explanation seemed to exhaust Tabby. She stopped by the vault and stood silently. Julie prompted her again: "And so you went in and saw Worth?"

"Yes. And I mentioned my concerns, and he just laughed. He said the Lincoln letter was the least of his worries. It was the muskets he was really upset by—his and the Society's. He said those were definitely gone, but that the Lincoln letter was probably safe."

"Safe? At his house?"

"No. That's what I was thinking, too."

"Where then?" Julie was tiring of the pace; would Tabby ever get to it?

"He said Jason has it."

"Jason?"

"That's what Worth said. He said he figured it all out, and Jason took the letters—the Lincoln one and the others."

"The Brigham Young letters? But we found those, here in the vault."

"But Worth didn't know that then," Tabby answered. "That's what's so confusing—Worth was so sure that Jason had taken all the letters, but knew you had found the Brigham Young papers. I just don't know what to think. Maybe Worth was wrong."

"What did he say, Tabby?"

"That he had figured it all out. Jason needed money. We all know he has that expensive car and house and, well, the way he lives. You just can't live like that on his salary. So Worth thought Jason took the letters before you got here—to take advantage of the transition. That's the way Worth put it—the transition. He said Jason couldn't have gotten away with the thefts when Worth was in charge, but it would take you some time to get to know the collections."

Julie was silent, trying to make sense of what Tabby was saying. Had Worth known something, or was he just guessing? Could Jason have been the thief? The murderer? But Tabby had been there; could she have killed him?

"Does that make any sense to you?" Tabby asked. She was in front of her desk now, and reached to pick up the letter opener she used for the doctor's correspondence.

"Well, it could," Julie replied. "Of course it could, but do you think Worth had any proof, any real evidence about Jason?"

"He didn't say any more. And now he's dead. Oh, dear!" Tabby began to sob. "What if Jason tries to kill me?"

"What are you talking about, Tabby?" Julie was having a hard time following.

"Jason could have done it."

"Killed Worth?"

"Yes. Don't you see? If Jason knew that Worth suspected him, Jason might have gone there after I left and killed him. And then he might try to—"

"To kill you, Tabby? Is that what you're afraid of?"

"Of everything! Do you think he knows what Worth told me? Do you think Worth told him I was there? That's why I didn't tell the police I had seen Worth on Sunday!" Tabby reached down to the desk for a tissue and blew her nose loudly. She was still holding the letter opener, which Julie eyed warily.

"About Sunday," Julie said as calmly as she could, trying not to set Tabby off again. "When did you leave Worth's house?"

"Three o'clock or so, I think."

"Did you tell your sister about this?"

"Martha? No. When I got home she wasn't there, and she didn't come home until suppertime, and she was in one of her moods. She gets a little hysterical sometimes and I know to just leave her alone. Anyway, I thought Worth would take care of things, get Jason to give the letters back. I didn't expect he'd be killed!"

Tabby struggled to regain her composure, and even though Julie didn't think she could have killed Worth, just being here alone with her made Julie anxious. Where was Rich? Julie wasn't wearing her watch. "Tabby, do you know what time it is?"

Tabby dabbed at her nose with her tissue and peered down at her left wrist to check her watch. "It's five-fifteen. Am I keeping you?"

"No, no, it's all right, I'm just expecting somebody," Julie assured her, smiling and breathing a sigh of relief. "Tabby, look, I'm sorry—I should have told you this before. The Lincoln letter has been found."

"Found? Where? Did Jason have it?" Tabby made one large sweep with the letter opener as she spoke.

"I can't really say because Chief Barlow is still investigating. But Tabby, you're right-handed, aren't you?" Julie had been watching Tabby wield that letter opener without quite realizing why she found it so significant—until she saw it was in Tabby's right hand.

"Why?"

"Just curious."

"Yes, I'm right-handed. I come from a family of left-handed people, but I was the odd one out. Martha always told me being left-handed was a sign of intelligence. She said that's why she liked Jason so much."

At the mention of his name, she looked like she was about to weep again.

"Do you mean that Jason is left-handed, too?"

Tabby nodded.

Thirty-two

Footsteps on the stairs stopped Julie from pursuing that thought. "That must be Rich," she said, and moved to the door to greet him.

"The outside door was open, so I let myself in and heard voices up here," Jason explained when Julie let out at gasp at seeing him enter the library.

"You're not supposed to be here!" she said.

"It's not up to Barlow whether or not I come to my office. You didn't say anything to me about that, although I guess you said plenty to Barlow."

As he was speaking, Jason advanced toward Julie, who stepped back and then realized she was directly in front of the open vault.

"What do you want, Jason?"

"Barlow wants me to meet with some detective from the State Police. My lawyer told me I'd need to be able to verify dates and times they might ask me about. So I needed my datebook. I came to get it; that okay with you, boss?"

"Mike asked you to stay away. So please go get your calendar and leave."

For a moment, Julie thought Jason would do just that, but then he advanced toward her again. She couldn't step away from him this time because she was now standing in the doorway of the vault. He noticed.

"You seem to have a thing for that vault," Jason said.

"Tabitha? Tabitha? Are you still up there?"

The woman's voice from the bottom of the steps halted Jason's advance. He stepped sideways and turned toward the door. Julie took advantage of his move to walk quickly toward Tabby's desk, where Tabby stood, frozen with fright.

"Tabitha?" the voice sounded again from below.

"It's your sister, Tabby," Julie said softly. "Tell her to come up."

But Tabby remained mute, clearly terrified. "We're up here, Martha," Julie called out. "Please come up."

What good Martha Preston might do Julie wasn't sure, but having someone else in the library seemed a good idea.

Martha surveyed the scene as she entered. "Quite a crowd," she said. "Did I interrupt a meeting?"

"No, I was just talking with your sister, and Jason came by to pick up something in his office. Go right ahead, Jason. We'll all come down and close up."

Jason paused but then started toward the door. "I'll do that," he said.

When he left, Tabby let out her breath. "Are you okay, dear?" her sister asked. Tabby responded with a nod but no words.

"You're looking a little pale. Let's get going."

"I'd rather wait till Jason leaves," Tabby said.

"I'm sure everything will be fine now, Tabby," Julie said.

"Whatever is the matter, dear?" Martha asked.

"Oh, Tabby was just saying she felt like she was coming down with something, right, Tabby?" Julie asked, and continued before Tabby could respond. "And how are you, Martha? I hope you're feeling better now, after Sunday."

At the question, the woman put her left hand across her chest and stared. "Sunday? You mean feeling better after Worth's death?"

"Of course not! Why would I think that," said Julie, knowing where she wanted to go but not sure how to get there. "Tabby mentioned earlier that you were upset about something on Sunday."

"I have no idea what Tabby said, Dr. Williamson, but I can assure you I wasn't ill. I went out for a long walk during the afternoon and I was quite tired. I believe I went to bed early, didn't I, Tabby?" Tabby nodded. "Really, we must be going now, dear, especially if you're not feeling well."

"Julie? Are you up there?"

Rich's voice came up the stairs, and Julie turned from the women and raced to the open door to answer. In seconds he was in the library. Julie hugged him tightly.

"What's going on?" asked Rich. "I practically got knocked down by Jason Battles when I was coming through the door. I was trying to read that Post-it note, and he pushed the door open in my face and tore out. Didn't even speak."

"I'll explain," Julie said.

Rich noticed the two women at the desk and released his grip of Julie.

"Rich O'Brian," she said quickly, "let me introduce two of our important volunteers—Tabby and Martha Preston. Tabby is our librarian, and Martha runs our gift shop."

As Rich moved toward them to shake hands, Martha added, "I'm also a trustee."

After quick handshakes, Martha said, "Now, Tabby, it is past time. We must be going. Nice to have met you, Mr. O'Brian. Good night."

Martha took her sister's arm and led her to the door. Julie and Rich stood at the top of the stairs and watched them go out the door.

"I'm so sorry I was late," Rich began as he embraced Julie, holding her more tightly now that they were without an audience. "There was an accident on the highway—a log truck rolled over, and everything was blocked in both directions."

"You got here just in time."

"What in the world was going on here?" he asked.

"It's a long story. Let's go down to my office and I'll tell you."

When they sat down beside the desk in her office, Julie suddenly felt very tired.

"You okay?" Rich asked.

"I just feel beat, wrung out, but I'm okay. I can't wait to tell you all this."

"What's all this?

Julie summarized what had happened in the library: Tabby's story about Worth Harding and his suspicion that Jason had taken both the Lincoln and Young letters; Tabby's right-handedness; Jason's appearance and her fear of him; and then Martha's arrival—and the revelation that both she and Jason were lefties.

"Your interest in lefties and righties is no doubt significant, Julie, but not to me."

She explained that Mike Barlow believed Worth's killer was left-handed.

"So you think Battles or Martha Preston killed him?" Rich asked.

"Exactly!"

"The puzzle-master strikes!" Rich said.

"Not exactly strikes, but I do feel like I'm zeroing in."

"You said both Martha and Battles could have killed Harding because they're lefties—but why?"

"With Jason it's pretty obvious: If Worth told Tabby Preston of his suspicions, he might have somehow let Jason know, and Jason could have killed him to prevent him from telling anyone else. But whether or not he did, I'm not sure, because Mike Barlow said Jason had an alibi for Sunday night—not a very strong one, and Mike still has to check that out."

"And Martha Preston?"

"Martha had the opportunity. Tabby said Martha didn't come home on Sunday until suppertime, and she said Martha was upset. Martha dismissed that, said she was just tired. As to why she would kill Worth, I don't know. I've told you there was something really funny about Martha and Worth. They always jabbed at each other at board meetings, and a couple of people hinted that there was some sort of relationship between them that went way back. But I just can't put my finger on it. And then Mary Ellen Swanson hinted that Martha had had some 'mental problems.' Maybe somehow that's all connected."

"You think Martha Preston and Worth Harding were lovers?"

Julie shrugged. "Anyway," she said, shaking her head as if clearing out something, "I guess we're not going to solve this now. And I think I need to call the police chief and tell—wait, I want to do something first."

Thirty-three

"You sure you should be doing this?" Rich asked as they stepped into Jason Battles's small office.

"Why not? All this belongs to the Ryland Historical Society, and I'm the director, so I can look at what's here."

"I guess you're right, legally, but I feel kind of funny—like we're invading his privacy."

"I'm not going to take anything, Rich. Just look around."

"For?"

"I don't know yet. Let's see."

She stood over the desk and made a quick inventory: computer disks, papers piled in neat stacks, pens, a couple of books. And Jason's calendar. "He said he was coming to get this!" Julie said.

"He must have forgotten. He was mad when he left, and obviously in a hurry. I'm sure he'll be back to get it."

But Julie was undeterred.

"Let's see what else is here," she said and began to poke among the papers. "Requests for visits, tour schedules, that sort of thing," she said as she regrouped the stack and returned it to its original position before picking up another and proceeding the same way. "It's all historical society stuff."

"What did you expect?"

"I don't know, but I keep thinking there may be other stuff here somewhere. Stuff he would have taken if he had stayed long enough to get his calendar. Maybe in here," she said and reached down to pull the large file drawer on the lower left side of Jason's desk. "It's locked!"

"That's not so strange, is it? Don't you lock your drawers?"

"I don't even have a key to my desk! Guess Mrs. Detweiller hasn't gotten around to giving me one."

"So you don't have a key to Jason's?"

"No, but maybe we could pry it open."

Julie quickly left the office, went to her own, and returned with one of the sticks used to block open the windows. Waving it as she reentered, she said, "Try this."

"I don't know, Julie."

"Go on, it's such an old desk, it should break easily."

Rich applied pressure slowly, and in a few seconds, they heard a click, and the drawer came loose. Julie let out a small cheer, reached into the file drawer and retrieved a stack of papers. “Brigham Young stuff—he was working on an article about that. Let’s see: an article from a history journal, some notes about Young’s travels in New England, and . . . copies of the correspondence. Every one of the thirteen letters!”

“So? You said he was working on an article.”

“Yes, but he said he had borrowed the originals from the vault to check them against what he was writing on his computer. But he has copies—he didn’t have to bring the originals here.”

“You don’t know when he made the copies, Julie. Maybe that was why he brought them down here in the first place.”

“But he didn’t say he’d copied them.”

“Maybe he didn’t want to get Tabby Preston mad. Isn’t she the copy guru?”

“True. But it’s still strange that he never said he had the copies. He just said he returned the originals after checking them against his work.”

Julie stacked the pile on top of the desk and reached into the drawer for another. She quickly turned the first few pages, and then stopped and said, “Wow!”

“What is it?” Rich asked and leaned in to see. “Looks like a printout from the Web.”

“It’s from eBay! So are these.”

She flipped through the next half-dozen sheets.

“Price information on Lincoln and Brigham Young letters!” she said triumphantly. “So Jason was checking out prices!”

“With everything going on around here, maybe he was just curious,” Rich said. “What are the dates?”

Julie smiled as she leafed through the sheets. "Last February. Long before the letters were found to be missing. And look at this!"

She handed Rich a thick bound booklet.

"An auction catalog," she explained. "From Maurice's company! What a coincidence."

Rich read out the title: "Important American Autographs and Correspondence." Then he opened the catalog to the two places marked with Post-it notes. "Are you surprised that he marked the pages for 'L' and 'Y'?"

"Not at all! I think we've got the last piece of the puzzle!"

With no warning, Jason appeared in the doorway.

"I suppose I shouldn't be surprised that you're rifling through my desk," he said.

He moved swiftly to the desk and reached for the last pile of papers, the ones with the auction catalog and eBay printouts. "These are mine, so I'll just take them now."

Rich stepped forward and grabbed Jason's left arm. "I don't think so," he said. Rich squeezed hard, and Jason dropped the papers back on the desk. The two men were facing each other.

"Why don't you just get your hands off me before I get mad?" Jason said, staring at Rich with a hard, cold look.

Rich kept his grip. "I'm not sure we're finished here," he said quietly, but with a firmness that Julie found both surprising and comforting. The athlete under the quiet professor—that was something Julie tended to forget about Rich. And something she was now very happy about.

The two men stared at each other. Julie didn't know who would give in, but she knew she had to do something.

"I'm going to call Mike Barlow," she said and grabbed the phone. She told the dispatcher she needed Chief Barlow at the

Ryland Historical Society. "Yes, it's an emergency," she said. "Please tell him to come right away."

"Let me go," said Jason. "Now!"

Julie picked up the window stick Rich had used to pry the desk drawer and handed it to him. "This might be useful," she said.

"You won't need that," Jason said. "I just want to sit down."

Rich looked at Julie. "Okay," she said.

Jason rubbed his arm and looked menacingly at Rich, but dropped into the chair at his desk. Rich remained behind him and held the window stick across his chest. Julie moved to the other side of the desk, between it and the door. "I think the chief can sort this out," she said, "but don't you think you owe me an explanation, Jason?"

"Julie, I think you should wait for the police," Rich interrupted. "Isn't that a siren?"

Julie heard it, too—the burping sound of the police siren, louder with each second as the cruiser approached. Of course she could wait, but she was so close.

"I mean, I gather you needed money and figured the Lincoln and Young letters would take care of that, but then to go from that to murder . . ."

"Murder!" Jason exclaimed. "I didn't kill Worth."

"Battles, what the hell are you doing here?" Mike Barlow roared as he rushed into the office.

The policeman turned and directed his question as much at Julie as at Jason, but it was the young man who responded: "She accused me of killing Worth. No way! That's crazy."

"Somebody tell me what's going on here. And who are you," he said, looking at Rich. Introductions were made, and Julie started to explain to Mike about finding the letters.

"I'll take over here now," Mike interrupted. "I appreciate your help. Mind if Battles and I stay here a few moments?"

"Rich and I can wait in my office," Julie said with obvious disappointment. "I have to close up when we're done."

"And set the security system," Mike said, and winked at her, a sign she read as "No hard feelings."

"Okay," Julie said excitedly as she closed her office door behind her and began to pace. Rich took a chair with a view of the Common.

"Okay what?" he asked.

Julie picked up another of the window sticks and jabbed it toward Rich as she spoke.

"First," she said, "we saw the copies of the letters, the eBay printouts, and the auction catalog. He was obviously checking prices. Second, putting the Young letters back in the 'L' box would explain why he closed me in the vault. Third, he tried to use the old security code to get in and replace the Lincoln letter, and when it didn't work he dropped the letter by the steps. Fourth . . ."

"Hey, stop pointing that at me, will you?" Rich said. "I left mine in the other room."

"Sorry. But it follows that—"

"Look!" Rich said and jumped up. He pointed through the window to the Common. Julie came to his side to see what he was looking at. "What's she doing out there?"

Before Julie could answer, Mike came into the office. "I've got to go," he said breathlessly. "Can you keep Jason Battles here? I just had a call. Something's . . . oh, God; there she is."

He joined them at the window. It was a bizarre scene. A woman was standing at the edge of the Common, swinging an iron skillet, and carrying on a one-sided conversation with no one in particular.

"I've got to get to her before she does something crazy. Stay with Battles. I cuffed him to the chair."

They hurried into the secretary's office and looked into Battles's office. He was seated, and his hands were held together with handcuffs looped around the arm of the chair.

The policeman rushed to the outside door.

"This shouldn't take long," he said.

"We can watch Battles from here," Rich said. "He'd have to carry that whole chair if he tried to move. And give me that stick."

Julie handed it to him, and Rich walked to the door of Jason's office and said something to him that Julie didn't hear. "He's going to stay right there," Rich said. "And what the hell's going on?"

"It's Martha Preston," Julie said, "and I think I know exactly what's going on . . . now."

Thirty-four

Julie watched Mike Barlow trot across the corner of the historical society's property toward the edge of the green area where Martha Preston stood. With the windows closed, Julie couldn't hear, so she reached down and pulled one open. Although Rich had the biggest of the blocking sticks, she found a shorter one and inserted it and then lowered herself to the floor so she could both watch and listen. Martha Preston was laughing maniacally and waving the skillet. Mike moved in beside her. He tried to grab her arm, but the woman twisted around and stood facing him. Julie thought she heard Martha say something about letters, but she was having trouble hearing clearly.

"I just have to get closer," she said out loud and then rushed back into the outer office.

"I'm going out," she told Rich. "You okay here?"

"Fine. But stay out of this, Julie. Or at least be careful," he added as he watched her run through the outside door. He shook his head.

As she approached the street directly across from where Mike Barlow and Martha Preston faced each other, she was aware of several people standing just down the street and, like her, watching intently the unfolding drama on the Common. Then out of the group Tabby Preston emerged, moving with a swiftness that surprised Julie, holding her dress as she broke into what could only be called a run.

"Martha!" Tabby yelled as she moved forward.

"Stay there," Barlow said sharply to Tabby. "Martha and I are just having a little talk."

"Those damned letters!" Martha's voice was easily heard now from where Julie stood. The woman began to swing the skillet again. Mike stepped back to avoid the circle of the swing.

"What letters?" Julie asked out loud.

Tabby was on the move again.

"Stay there!" the policeman said again in Tabby's direction, but Tabby kept moving.

Julie ran across the street to join Tabby on the Common.

"Come over here," she said gently as she took Tabby's arm and directed her away. "Mike can handle this." Julie felt Tabby giving in, and she walked her a few yards away, toward the street.

"I had no idea," Tabby said. "No idea at all. I still can't believe it."

"Can't believe what?" Julie asked in the calmest tone she could muster.

"That Martha . . . that Martha . . ."

"That Martha killed Worth," Julie completed the sentence.

"Yes—because of those silly letters."

But that's not possible, Julie said to herself. Jason Battles took the letters. So why were Martha and Tabby going on about letters?

Before Julie could consider the matter further, she heard Mike's gentle voice. "That's fine, Martha. I'll just take that now. It's pretty heavy, isn't it?"

Julie saw that the policeman now held the skillet in one hand and was using the other to grip Martha's shoulder. The woman looked as if she would collapse without Mike's support.

"Let's just walk over here now, Martha," Mike continued very calmly as he walked Martha to where Julie and Tabby stood.

"Get Tabby out of here," he said sharply to Julie.

Julie felt she was pushing Tabby. The woman seemed so thin, but to Julie, moving her along toward the historical society's campus felt like propelling a barrel or a heavy chest. If Tabby was a big blue heron, she wasn't about to propel herself with her own wings. When they finally got there and Rich met them at the door, Julie flashed him a look that he instantly understood to mean "Don't say a word." So he just nodded as the two women went into Julie's office. She had to talk to Tabby now.

When they were done talking—when Tabby was simply unable to say more and sat like a limp doll in the chair by the desk—Julie went out to get her a glass of water. Rich sat at Mrs. Detweiller's desk.

"What's going on out here?"

"Well," said Rich, "considering that Battles was cuffed to the chair, I didn't need to use my weapon here," he said, playfully brandishing the window stick. "A state trooper came and took him. And Barlow took Martha to the hospital."

"That's the right place for her; she should have been there long before now, according to what I've just learned from her sister."

"Which is . . ."

"Let me just get Tabby her glass of water and then I'll tell you everything."

"Did you hear Martha yelling about letters?" Julie asked Rich when she returned.

"Yeah, what was that all about?"

"Martha killed Worth because—"

"Wait a minute! Martha Preston killed him? What about Battles?"

"He just took the letters. The two things weren't connected at all."

"So why were the old ladies talking about letters?"

"Martha and Worth had been a couple when they were teenagers, and then he broke it off and she never got over him. When she moved back to Ryland, she wanted to take up with him again, but Worth didn't. That's why she was always picking at him in meetings, I guess. I told you they had a weird relationship."

"You did. But I'm still lost about the letters."

"Over the years, after she left town, she wrote to him. Lots of love letters, I guess you'd call them. But since she's been back and Worth didn't show any interest in resuming their relationship, she became more and more anxious about the letters. Tabby said when Martha learned he was leaving his house to the historical society, she must have gotten scared I'd find the letters. Then, to top it all off, Worth announced he was writing a memoir, and Martha really flipped out. She didn't want anyone to know he had rejected her—even though everyone in town pretty much knew already—or to read the letters. Tabby said Martha was probably scared to death that she'd have to resign in disgrace from the board of trustees, or that people would make fun of her. Can you imagine—all because of a relationship that happened more than forty years ago? But then Tabby also said that Martha has had quite a few mental breakdowns over the years, and she often blows things way out of proportion. She's still not stable, is how Tabby put it."

"Sad really," Rich said. "What a burden to bear. It almost sounds as if Harding was tormenting her."

"It does sort of seem that way, but who knows. Tabby didn't know about the letters before today, when Martha told her everything. Martha was apparently out for a walk on Sunday and saw Tabby leaving Worth's. She probably thought Worth was telling Tabby about the love letters, or maybe she was jealous. Anyway, I don't know exactly what happened—I'm not sure Tabby really does, either. But Martha obviously went to Worth's house after Tabby left and killed him with a skillet."

"God, what a tale!"

"Amazing, isn't it? And here's something else Martha said to Tabby: 'Worth tried to steal our history.'"

"And he wasn't the only one stealing history. Jason was, too."

"And two guys from somewhere stole muskets," she added.

"And what about the Klan robe? Did Jason steal that, too?"

"You mean, you didn't sweat that out of him when you had him tied up and you had the club to beat him?" Julie said.

"I forgot."

"Okay, but just try to do better next time." She laughed, and he joined in.

"I've got to find somone to stay with Tabby tonight, but when that's done, I just want to go home. With you. You're staying tonight, aren't you?"

"No. Thought I'd just leave and then start calling you and hanging up when you answer."

"Give me that stick," Julie said.

Thirty-five

When they got to the condo, Rich poured her a glass of wine and settled her into a chair in the kitchen.

"Now you can watch me and learn how to make an omelet," he said.

From far back in her mind Julie pulled out the memory of having eaten eggs for breakfast—could that really have been just this morning?—but decided she could handle the cholesterol.

When the phone rang, Julie picked up. She put her hand over the mouthpiece and whispered "It's Mike" and took the portable phone into the living room. Rich removed the pan of beaten eggs from the stove and followed her. She had already hung up when he joined her.

"He's coming right over," Julie said. "Maybe you can make a bigger omelet."

"Eggs twice in the same day," Mike Barlow said as he sat down with Julie and Rich.

"Julie and I had breakfast this morning," he explained to Rich.

"Really?" Rich said, as he looked at Mike.

"It doesn't seem like the same day, does it?" Julie asked. "So, what is happening?"

"Why don't we start with what you know," Mike answered.

When Julie finished, Mike said, "I don't know why the Town of Ryland bothers to pay me. You seem to have things in hand."

Julie blushed. "But there's one thing you missed earlier," the policeman continued. "Don't want you to feel too proud."

"What did I miss?"

"About the gloves. Remember when I said that whoever killed Worth might have planned it because he brought gloves?"

"Yes. So?"

"Martha didn't have to bring gloves. She was wearing them—lots of ladies her age do, especially on Sundays. At least here in Ryland."

"I remember the first time I met her," Julie said. "She wore gloves to the trustees meeting. I couldn't believe it. But anyway, that means she didn't plan it. It just happened."

"Probably right."

"How is she?"

"Not good, I'd say. I figured Community Hospital was a better place than the county jail. She's sedated. God only knows what'll happen when that wears off, but they'll watch her closely. And, I've talked to the District Attorney about her and Battles, so it's really out of my hands now."

"Surely Martha won't have to stand trial," Julie said.

"I can't see her being tried either, but like I said, it's up to the DA."

"And Jason?"

"Also up to the DA. He basically admitted everything to me. All that stuff you found in his desk was pretty hard for him to explain away. So his case should go to trial, unless he pleads out. He also admitted that he made the phone calls—and locked you in the vault."

"Did he say why?"

"He said that morning he noticed Tabby Preston left the library to go downstairs, so he figured it was a good chance to return the Brigham Young letters—since you'd reported them missing, he couldn't take the chance of trying to sell them. So he went upstairs and opened the vault and put the letters back—in the 'L' box—and was ready to leave when he heard someone coming up the stairs. When he saw it was you, he dropped down behind Tabby's desk."

"So he *was* there?" Julie shuddered as she visualized the scene, Jason lurking, then rushing to slam the door shut—with her inside. "I don't know why I didn't see him. I guess I was just so surprised about the vault being open. But why did he lock me in?"

"He claims he wasn't thinking. He was going to try to slip away, but then he heard Tabby coming up the stairs. So he closed the vault door quickly so she wouldn't know he had been in there. He said he figured if Tabby didn't reopen it, he could think of an excuse and do it right away and get you out. But then he heard you and that was his excuse."

"And the phone calls?" Rich asked.

"Well, Jason Battles is not completely wrapped when it comes to women. I didn't think I should say anything before, but I'll just say now that he's had some run-ins before—a stalking complaint from one girl, and a charge from another that was ultimately withdrawn. That's why I was suspicious, and when the calls stopped after he overheard you talking to the phone company about caller ID, that clinched it."

"So it all comes together," Julie said. She was visualizing a puzzle, a huge complicated jigsaw puzzle with all the pieces now neatly fit together.

"Wait a minute," she said, "what about the Klan robe?"

"I asked him," Mike said, "but he was adamant. He didn't think the Klan robe had any value. No, it was just the letters he wanted."

"Like Martha," Julie said. "Isn't it funny that Worth's murder really was about letters after all."

Mike nodded and took the last bite of his omelet.

"This is great, Rich. You could get a job at The Greek if teaching gets boring."

Rich passed his quizzical look first to Mike and then to Julie, who explained about the diner.

"Are you satisfied about the painting?" Mike continued. "I mean, that it was really just misplaced?"

"I think so," Julie answered. "Any of the volunteers might have done it to be helpful—to refresh the room, to protect the painting from light, whatever. I'll definitely follow up on that, but the point is, the painting's safe."

"So it wasn't connected to the rest?" Rich asked.

"Probably a red herring, like you said the other day, but an accidental one."

"Guess so," Rich said, and paused before continuing. "The one thing that still bothers me is how those guys who took the muskets knew they were in Harding's house? And how did they do it—get in and take them without his knowing?"

"I think I can answer the first question," Julie replied. "I just saw this old brochure that described the Society's muskets. They must have seen that somewhere and decided to try to get them. They must have been pretty disappointed when they found out the muskets weren't on display, but somehow they found out they were at Worth's. Maybe they talked to a volunteer, or maybe even to Worth himself."

"But how did they get them?" Rich asked again.

"Maybe we'll find out if they get caught," Barlow said. "If we get them. If not, well, that's another piece that we can't fit in the puzzle."

"They probably just walked right into the house," Julie said. "He said he often didn't lock his house."

"So that's what I'd guess: the house was unlocked, they got in and jimmied the locks on the cabinet. They were pros, after all, so they would have had the right tools," Mike said. "We may never know. Sometimes . . ."

Julie finished for him. "The pieces aren't all there."

"Right. Well, I hate to eat and run," Mike said, "but I need to go write up my reports. Thanks for dinner, Rich. And for all your help, Julie."

As they were getting into bed an hour later, Rich said, "You seem agitated. I thought you'd be settled now that everything's figured out."

"Not quite everything. What about the Klan robe?"

Thirty-six

With the heat wave broken, Ryland moved into several days of delightful weather—bright, clear days with temperatures in the low seventies and refreshingly cool nights. The past two days had been too hectic for Julie to think about the weather, but this night, even with Rich joining her, she delighted in pulling up an extra blanket against the evening chill. The result was a deeply appealing cocoon, one she felt, as the dawn drew her toward modest consciousness, that she'd be happy to stay in for a long time.

But then the phone rang.

"Sorry for the wake-up call," Mike Barlow said. "When it's convenient," he continued, "could you drop by the station?"

Julie showed up at the Ryland town office a little before eight, going around to the back door with the RYLAND POLICE sign. Funny that after all this involvement with Mike Barlow, this was her first visit to the station. He greeted her as she came through the door. "I really am sorry about calling so early," he said, "but I figured you'd want to know this. Come in and sit down while I get us some coffee. Black, right?"

"Is it about Martha?" Julie asked as she cradled her mug.

"No, nothing more on that front. She's still in the hospital. Here's a hint: any property still missing from the Ryland Historical Society?"

"The Klan outfit?" Julie asked.

"No longer missing." Mike rose and left the office. He returned with a plastic trash bag and presented it to Julie with mock ceremony.

Julie reached for it and extracted enough of the robe to realize it was indeed a Ku Klux Klan outfit.

"Where did it turn up?"

"Right where it belongs, in my opinion—the Ryland dump. Or, I should give it the proper name: our regional recycling center. Ever been there?"

"Not yet, but I've got lots of moving boxes to take there for recycling."

"Well, when you go, you'll meet Riley Warner—the attendant. He checks through all the recyclables to make sure you've sorted the bottles from the cans and the newspapers from the magazines. Riley stopped by last evening while I was working on my report. Seems someone dropped off this bag yesterday, and of course he checked it."

"Did he see who left it?"

"Matter of fact, he did."

"And?"

"You want to sit down?"

"No. Just tell me, Mike!"

When Mary Ellen Swanson entered Julie's office and saw the Klan outfit draped across a chair, she gasped and immediately sat down.

"I can't tell you how deeply ashamed I am. I should have realized nosy old Riley Warner would have checked the bag—he looks for items to sell, I believe. Anyway, I should have known. Oh, dear, Julia, I do feel so utterly awful about this."

"Julie," Julie quickly corrected her. "Yes, I'm sure you do, but all I'm interested in is an explanation."

"My husband's family has been in Ryland since the Revolutionary War, as I'm sure you know. And terribly proud of being First Families and all. Being here so long, they naturally reflected the history of the town, and I'm afraid that's for the bad as well as the good. Dan's father—also named Dan; we called him Old Dan to keep them straight—apparently got caught up in the anti-French movement in the twenties."

"And joined the Klan?"

"I'm not really sure he was a member. My husband never said so directly, but the fact is, we had this old stuff in the attic along with a lot of Old Dan's things. My husband gave it to Worth; this was probably ten years or so ago. I don't have any idea what he told Worth, but I'm sure Worth put two and two together and realized it was my father-in-law's."

"As a matter of fact," Julie said, "there isn't any indication on the inventory card about the source of the outfit."

"I'm sure Worth was being discreet, but frankly, it bothered me a great deal. Then when my husband died and I decided to support the new wing in his honor, I got to thinking about the Klan robe and how badly it reflected on the family. I planned to talk to Worth about it before he left the job and you came, but we never got around to it. Then when the whole business about doing an inventory came up, I was afraid you'd find the Klan robe and Worth would mention my husband, and . . ."

"As you said, you were ashamed."

"Yes. So I decided to remove it. It really didn't have any value, you know."

"And that's why you voted against the resolution to have the inventory done," Julie said. "I never understood that."

"Abstained," Swanson corrected her. "In any case, I don't know why I thought my little vote would slow things down, but I just couldn't bring myself to vote for the inventory and have you discover the Klan robe. It would reflect so badly on my husband's family, just at the time I was trying to memorialize them with the building."

"And so you took it."

"Yes. It wasn't really hard. I came in the day after the vote on the inventory and told one of the volunteers I was bringing in an old dress to add to the costume collection. If you're a trustee, they tend to let you do what you like. So I just exchanged the dress for the Klan outfit. It was very simple."

"But you waited quite a while to get rid of it."

"Yes. I was quite conflicted, dear. I kept it around, thinking I might bring it to you and explain, but then with things going missing all over the place, it seemed like a good opportunity just to get rid of that damned thing. So I took it to the dump yesterday. I should have realized Riley would be watching. I'm sorry."

"I guess the thing is, it's back now," Julie said. "And everything else is accounted for."

"Really?" Swanson asked.

"Yes, it's quite a long story, and I'll put together an explanation for the board as soon as I get time, but the fact is, all the mysteries are solved now."

"Including Worth's murder, I understand. Poor Martha! I mean, I knew she had some problems, but this . . ."

"I'm not really able to talk about all this, Mary Ellen. I'm sure the news will get out soon—or I guess it already has."

"We're a small community here in Ryland, Julie."

"Yes, well anyway, the point about the Klan outfit is that it was the last piece of the puzzle, and now it's solved."

"I do feel I should resign, don't you?" Swanson asked abruptly.

"Resign?"

"From the board of trustees. I don't see how you can have me on it when I've stolen something from the Society."

"Mary Ellen, I'd hate to have you leave the board because of this little matter. I think we can just let it be something between us. And I'm sure Mike Barlow isn't interested in it."

"That's so very kind of you, dear. I would like to carry on as a trustee, for my husband's family's sake. And, of course, the new building will bear my husband's name."

"Of course." Julie stopped speaking so she could wrestle with her thoughts—of course what Mary Ellen had done was absolutely wrong, even if understandable, but Julie also recognized the woman's generosity. Her gift, after all, was making possible the new Swanson addition—they had only to raise an additional $200,000 to finish funding it.

As if reading Julie's mind, Mary Ellen said, "I realize we still have a gap to fill on that. I was thinking about helping a bit more, in fact. What I was thinking was that if I added another $100,000 as a challenge, perhaps the board could hold a matching fundraiser to complete the project. What do you think, dear? Would that be helpful?"

Thirty-seven

Standing in the open door, Mrs. Detweiller cleared her throat. "Sorry to bother you, but I need to know what to do."

Whoa, Julie thought; this was a switch.

"About the library," the secretary continued. "Jason isn't here, and Tabby Preston hasn't come in yet—it's well past her usual time, so I called her. She says she's not coming in today. I just need to know if I should put up a sign saying the library's closed today."

"Yes, that's a good idea, Mrs. Detweiller. And Jason won't be in . . . well, for a bit. Maybe you could help me figure out what he would be doing for the next few days so I can cover for him."

Mrs. Detweiller returned with the information. Only one tour today, Julie was relieved to see; she felt she could readily handle that. Mrs. Detweiller lingered in the doorway.

"Anything else?" Julie asked.

"I just wanted to say, Dr. Williamson, that Martha's situation is quite shocking. Oh, it was terrible the way she kept pushing herself on Worth. I see a lot from where I sit, and I can tell you that Martha really went too far. Everyone who grew up here knew those two had been an item a long time ago, but when Martha came back to town, she just seemed to act like all those years away were nothing. It was ridiculous. She wanted to take up where they'd left off, and Worth didn't. But nobody, including myself, thought she'd ever go this far. And poor Worth . . ."

Mrs. Detweiller was actually getting a little choked up, much to Julie's surprise.

"Well, I've said my piece." Mrs. Detweiller said. "I just didn't want you or anyone to think I was aware of the, well, the intensity of Martha's delusions and failed to do anything about it."

She quickly left Julie's office. Leave it to Mrs. Detweiller, Julie thought, to make this all about being negligent in her secretarial duties.

Maybe it was the extra bounce that came from having it all over, or maybe it was because with Jason out of the picture Julie was ready to take on more of the daily work of the Society—or maybe it was just because she was a very good guide. Whatever the reason, the tour Julie gave that afternoon was dazzling. She could tell from the looks on the faces of the high school students and their teachers, faces that at the beginning reflected boredom but that were lighted up when she was finished. She had really turned them on to history. Julie felt she was floating as she made her way back to the office. The only small cloud now was Worth's house: Could she really live there if and when the Society got it? Could she somehow put away that image of his body on the floor and the blood beside it? Well, she'd face that problem when the time came, she decided.

"She just came in," Mrs. Detweiller was saying as Julie came through the door. "Please hold. It's for you, Dr. Williamson. A Maurice Leary."

"If you have a few minutes, Maurice, I can fill you in," Julie said when she had settled into her chair with the phone.

"Sounds interesting," Maurice Leary said. "Fire away."

"Let's start with the Lincoln letter," Julie said. "I think that's where you came in."

About the Author

William D. Andrews spent summers in Maine with his family for eighteen years until he could find a job to justify a permanent move. That happened in 1989 when he became president of Westbrook College in Portland. The merger of Westbrook and the University of New England freed him to pursue a lifelong interest in writing, supplemented by freelance editing and consulting for nonprofit organizations. Andrews has published three textbooks on management communications. He earned his bachelor's degree from the University of Pittsburgh and an MBA and doctorate from the University of Pennsylvania.

Andrews now divides his time between homes in Newry and Portland. He served as a trustee of the Bethel Historical Society (which is quite unlike the fictional Ryland Historical Society!), and remains active in the Society and the Mahoosuc Land Trust. He reads, skies, snowshoes, cooks and plays tennis.